FAIR BALL

FAIR BALL

DEREK JETER

with Paul Mantell

JETER CHILDREN'S

SIMON & SCHUSTER BOOKS FOR YOUNG READERS

New York   London   Toronto   Sydney   New Delhi

SIMON & SCHUSTER BOOKS FOR YOUNG READERS
An imprint of Simon & Schuster Children's Publishing Division
1230 Avenue of the Americas, New York, New York 10020
This book is a work of fiction. Any references to historical events, real people, or real places are used fictitiously. Other names, characters, places, and events are products of the author's imagination, and any resemblance to actual events or places or persons, living or dead, is entirely coincidental.

For information about special discounts for bulk purchases, please contact Simon & Schuster Special Sales at 1-866-506-1949 or business@simonandschuster.com.
The Simon & Schuster Speakers Bureau can bring authors to your live event. For more information or to book an event, contact the Simon & Schuster Speakers Bureau at 1-866-248-3049 or visit our website at www.simonspeakers.com.
Also available in a Simon & Schuster Books for Young Readers hardcover edition
Book design by Krista Vossen
The text for this book was set in Centennial LT Std.
Manufactured in the United States of America
0318 OFF
First Simon & Schuster Books for Young Readers paperback edition April 2018
2 4 6 8 10 9 7 5 3 1
The Library of Congress has cataloged the hardcover edition as follows:
Names: Jeter, Derek, 1974– author. | Mantell, Paul, author.
Title: Fair ball / Derek Jeter with Paul Mantell.
Description: First edition. | New York : Simon & Schuster Books for Young Readers, [2017] | "Jeter Children's." | Summary: "Derek is juggling finals and a baseball tournament during the last few weeks of school, but when his friend Dave starts ignoring him, Derek's perfect summer starts to look less fun"—Provided by publisher.
Identifiers: LCCN 2016040088| ISBN 9781481491488 (hardback) | ISBN 9781481491495 (paperback) | ISBN 9781481491501 (eBook)
Subjects: LCSH: Jeter, Derek, 1974-—Childhood and youth—Juvenile fiction. | CYAC: Jeter, Derek, 1974-—Childhood and youth—Fiction. | Baseball—Fiction. | Friendship—Fiction. | Prejudices—Fiction. | BISAC: JUVENILE FICTION / Social Issues / Friendship. | JUVENILE FICTION / Sports & Recreation / Baseball & Softball. | JUVENILE FICTION / Social Issues / Values & Virtues.
Classification: LCC PZ7.J55319 Fai 2017 | DDC [Fic]—dc23
LC record available at https://lccn.loc.gov/2016040088

To the Jeter's Leaders,
who embrace what makes each of us
unique and dedicate their lives to being
role models in their communities
—D. J.

A Note About the Text

The rules of Little League followed in this book are the rules of the present day. There are six innings in each game. Every player on a Little League baseball team must play at least two innings of every game in the field and have at least one at bat. In any given contest, there is a limit on the number of pitches a pitcher can throw, in accordance with age. Pitchers who are eight years old are allowed a maximum of fifty pitches in a game, pitchers who are nine or ten years old are allowed seventy-five pitches per game, and pitchers who are eleven or twelve years old are allowed eighty-five pitches.

Dear Reader,

Fair Ball is inspired by some of my experiences growing up. The book portrays the values my parents instilled in me and the lessons they have taught me about how to remain true to myself and embrace the unique differences in everyone around me.

Fair Ball is based on the lesson that the world isn't always fair. This is one of the principles I have lived by in order to achieve my dreams. I hope you enjoy reading!

Derek Jeter

DEREK JETER'S 10 LIFE LESSONS

1. Set Your Goals High (*The Contract*)

2. Think Before You Act (*Hit & Miss*)

3. Deal with Growing Pains (*Change Up*)

4. **The World Isn't Always Fair** (*Fair Ball*)

5. Find the Right Role Models

6. Don't Be Afraid to Fail

7. Have a Strong Supporting Cast

8. Be Serious but Have Fun

9. Be a Leader, Follow the Leader

10. Life Is a Daily Challenge

CONTRACT FOR DEREK JETER

1. Family Comes First. Attend our nightly dinner.
2. Be a Role Model for Sharlee. (She looks to you to model good behavior.)
3. Do Your Schoolwork and Maintain Good Grades (As or Bs).
4. Bedtime. Lights out at nine p.m. on school nights.
5. Do Your Chores. Take out the garbage, clean your room on weekends, and help with the dishes.
6. Respect Others. Be a good friend, classmate, and teammate. Listen to your teachers, coaches, and other adults.
7. Respect Yourself. Take good care of your body and your mind. Avoid alcohol and drugs. Surround yourself with positive friends with strong values.
8. Work Hard. You owe it to yourself and those around you to give your all. Do your best in everything that you do.
9. Think Before You Act.

Failure to comply will result in the loss of playing sports and hanging out with friends. Extra-special rewards include attending a Major League Baseball game, choosing a location for dinner, and selecting another event of your choice.

CONTENTS

FAIR BALL

Chapter One

PLAYOFFS!

"Stee-rike ONE!"

Derek Jeter winced as he stared at home plate from the on-deck circle. His teammate, Dean O'Leary, had just let a very hittable pitch go right by him. The odds of getting another meatball like that were slim to none. After all, it was the sixth inning already, and there was still no score for either team.

Both the Dodgers' pitcher and Dave Hennum, the Indians' hurler (and one of Derek's best friends), were at the top of their game. Neither team had gotten a runner past second base all day. If this game went into extra innings, both sides would have to reach for a relief pitcher.

It was the first game of the Westwood Little League

playoffs. This year the league had restructured the play-offs. The top four teams were now playing each other in a round-robin. The top two finishers would go head-to-head for the league championship.

But that wasn't all. In a new twist designed by the town, the winner of that game would then play the champion of the East Side league, for the first annual Kalamazoo Trophy!

The new format would make for four weeks of tension and excitement—*if* the Indians got that far. In his heart Derek was sure his team would win it all, including the Kalamazoo Trophy. With his dad as their coach, how could they not?

But Derek also knew that they still had to win the games, one by one. A loss to the Dodgers today would not knock them out of contention. But it might prove a fatal blow to their hopes in the end, so every at bat was important.

"Stee-rike TWO!" Dean had swung, but the pitch had already landed in the catcher's mitt.

This Dodgers pitcher was a real fireballer. Derek remembered him from the regular season. The Indians had won that game 6–5 but hadn't scored at all in this guy's four innings on the mound. And so far today the Indians' batters hadn't even sniffed him.

Derek swung his bat rhythmically in the on-deck circle, getting ready for his turn. He blew out regular, big breaths, trying to stay relaxed and calm.

The next pitch to Dean was in the dirt, and he almost swung at it. But the ump held his arms out in the "safe" sign, ruling that Dean had checked his swing.

The count was now 1–2, with one out and nobody on. "Protect, protect," Derek muttered under his breath, hoping Dean could read his thoughts and would make sure to swing at anything that was close to a strike.

The pitch came in. Dean watched it go by—right over the heart of the plate and down at the knees!

"Stee-rike three!" yelled the ump.

"What?" Dean cried, throwing his hands up. "That pitch was low!"

"Yer *out!*" the ump said. "Let's go. Next batter." Dean dragged himself away, groaning with frustration as he passed Derek on his way back to the bench.

Derek shook his head in sympathy, but he knew that Dean should have swung. The pitch might have been a little low, but it had been too close to let go by with two strikes. You never knew when an ump might miss a call. If you had to go down, it was better to go down swinging.

Derek set his feet in the batter's box. He could hear his teammates cheering him on. The Indians had learned over the course of their season to pull together as a unit and to play for one another, not just for themselves.

That was a tribute to their coaches. Derek's dad and Coach Bradway had made good players, such as Mason Adams, Jonathan Hogue, and Tito Ortega, better, and they'd made weaker players, such as Gary Parnell, Miles Kaufman, and Derek's good buddy Vijay Patel, play to the best of their abilities.

The Indians might not have been the most talented team in the league, but here they were in the playoffs—and Derek was convinced that this was only the beginning.

He had been named their regular-season MVP. If anyone was going to be able to hit the fastest pitcher they'd faced all season, he thought, it was probably him.

Derek rubbed some dirt onto his hands to get a better grip on the bat and dug his toes in to get the best possible footing. He pointed the bat straight at the pitcher, as a reminder to himself to try to hit the fastball straight up the middle, and not swing too hard in a useless effort to pull the ball.

Here came the pitch, and Derek was ready. The fastball was over the heart of the plate, and Derek's bat was there to meet it.

CRACK! The pitcher ducked. The ball was hit so hard that the center fielder couldn't get into position before it skidded right by him.

Derek was almost to first base when he saw that happen, and immediately he was thinking triple. He rounded second, barely touching it with the outside of his right foot, and slid into third just in time.

Now it was all up to Dave. Derek clapped and yelled encouragement along with the rest of the Indians. Dave had all kinds of power, but he struck out a lot because his swing was like a golf swing—up and down and under the ball.

There was good reason for that. Dave had started playing golf as a young kid, and he played whenever he got the chance. His dream was to be a professional golfer. He'd learned baseball only a year before, with Derek doing most of the teaching.

Derek knew Dave would have a hard time hitting this pitcher. Derek had a feeling that if he wanted to score, he was going to have to do it on his own. So when he saw the 1–1 pitch hit the dirt and get away from the catcher, he took off, trying to steal home.

The catcher, who was just picking up the ball, saw Derek barreling toward him. Startled, he lost his grip, and by the time he wheeled around to make the tag, it was too late.

"SAFE!" called the ump, stretching his arms out wide. And just like that, Derek had stolen the lead for his team.

Dave proceeded to strike out, just as Derek had feared. Now it was the Dodgers' turn for last licks. Dave was still on the mound, as he had been all game. He had been dominating the Dodgers hitters too, thanks to the wicked changeup that Derek had taught him early in the season.

Dave quickly fell behind the first hitter, 3–0. Derek didn't know how many pitches Dave had already thrown, but it was easy to see that his friend was tired. He knew that if Dave didn't get through this inning quickly, he'd reach his pitch limit. Derek snuck a peek at Coach Bradway, who was keeping the pitch count. He also happened to be Dave's guardian, the person who looked after him whenever Dave's parents were away on business—which was a whole lot. Chase (he liked to be called by his first name) was also the family's driver. The Hennum family was rich—richer than anyone Derek or his other friends had ever known. After all, not everybody could afford their own driver.

After a called strike the hitter lofted a long fly ball to right. Vijay was out there, but he looked uncomfortable as he settled under the ball. The sun must have been in his eyes, because he ducked at the last moment.

The ball hit his glove, then popped back up into the air. Derek held his breath for one endless instant, until Vijay recovered his wits and, mercifully, caught the ball a second time before it hit the ground.

Well, that's one out, at least, thought Derek. The next hitter lined the first pitch right at Dave, who at least managed to knock it down. It ricocheted off his glove over to Derek, who threw to first for the second out.

"Thanks!" Dave told him, relieved.

"Hey, what are friends for?" Derek said, and laughed.

Dave had to get just one more out—and he did, when the hitter swung at a 2–0 fastball and hit a fly ball to Gary Parnell in left, who put it away for the final out.

Game over. 1–0, Indians! The team had made Derek's

stolen run pay off. They were now 1–0 in the playoffs. As far as Derek was concerned, it was going to be clear sailing from here on in, all the way to the Kalamazoo Trophy!

"Hey, Dave," Derek said as the two of them helped pack up the team's gear, "don't forget about next weekend."

"Not a chance!" Dave said with a big grin.

For weeks the two boys had been planning a big overnight at Derek's house. "You can come over right after the game," Derek offered. "My folks said that whenever you come is good."

"Cool. I just have to check with my folks, and we're good to go."

"Awesome!" Derek was happy and excited as he got into the car with his dad and Vijay for the drive back to Mount Royal Townhouses, where both the Jeters and the Patels lived.

It was early June. Summer was almost here. Soon he'd be vacationing with his grandparents, spending his summer on Greenwood Lake in New Jersey, and going to Yankees games with his grandma. Best of all, his team was going to win the Kalamazoo Trophy!

Oh, and the cherry on top? He and Dave were finally going to have their long-planned overnight at Derek's.

For once in his life there wasn't the ghost of a problem on the horizon, Derek told himself. Other than the team possibly losing next week—which wasn't going to happen. What could possibly go wrong?

Chapter Two

THE BEST-LAID PLANS

"Come on, Dad. You *know* we're going to win that trophy."

Derek's dad looked at him sternly from across the dining room table, where the family was seated for dinner. "Cut that out. Are you *trying* to jinx us?"

"Come on, Dad. You're not superstitious, are you?"

"Who says I'm not?" Mr. Jeter kept a straight face, but he wasn't fooling anybody. Everyone in the family knew when he was joking and when he wasn't.

"Besides, it's not just a matter of the coaches doing a good job," Derek's father went on. "If we're going to get very far, you players have to bring your best effort every single game."

"You know *I* will, Dad. You won't have to worry about me."

"No, I don't worry about you. But I am afraid that some of the guys will be distracted, what with the end of school coming up, and summer just around the corner."

"Plus there's finals," Derek said.

"Well, I wouldn't want them to sacrifice studying. That's their most important job right now. But hopefully they've still got some time left for practice. Speaking of which, how's it going with *your* studying, Derek?"

"Fine." Derek had put in two hours already today, and two the day before. He hadn't even had time to get out and play ball on Jeter's Hill, the small green space in Mount Royal Townhouses where he and his friends played ball whenever they got the chance.

"Daddy, *I* don't have any finals," said Derek's sister, Sharlee, who had been listening, while scarfing down her mac and cheese.

"Well, aren't you lucky?" said Mrs. Jeter.

Yeah, Derek thought glumly. Sharlee was lucky, all right. Things were so simple when you were in first grade.

"It's not fair," he complained, half-joking. "I've got all this work to do. I've been hitting the books every single day for the past two weeks!"

His mom and dad smiled and exchanged a wink. "Good for you, old man," Mrs. Jeter said.

"You won't be sorry," added his dad.

Derek wasn't really jealous. He loved Sharlee, and the two of them got along very well most of the time. Still, it hurt to be chained to his books right now, just when the Indians were getting so close to glory.

"So, since my T-ball season is over and I don't have any finals, can I take karate class?" Sharlee suddenly said. "Ciara's doing it. Can I do it too? *Please? Pretty please?*"

Ciara had been Sharlee's best friend ever since the beginning of the school year. Everything either of them did, the other wanted to do.

"Oh, I don't see how you could," Mrs. Jeter said. "Remember, Sharlee, you and Derek are leaving for Grandma and Grandpa's house right after July Fourth, and you'll be gone six whole weeks. I don't want you starting something and then dropping out a month later."

"But, Mommy, this is a one-month class!" Sharlee cried. "See?" She took a piece of paper out of her jeans pocket and handed it to her mother.

"'One-month free-trial beginners' class,'" Mrs. Jeter read. "Well. That certainly is convenient. What do you think, Jeter?"

Mr. Jeter thought for a moment, then said, "I don't see why not, Dot. Sharlee needs something to do between now and New Jersey."

"Woo-hoo!" Sharlee exulted, doing a happy dance in her chair.

"And goodness knows she needs an outlet for all that energy," Mrs. Jeter said. "Not to mention that it's free. Can't beat the price, huh?"

Derek winced. He would have liked to try karate him-self, but he knew his parents wouldn't go for it. They would point out that there were finals to study for, and that his baseball team was in the playoffs, and ask him how he planned to balance all those things. He decided not to even ask. The more he thought about it, the more he realized that it wouldn't be a good idea to split his focus any further.

"Oh!" said Mrs. Jeter suddenly. "That reminds me, Derek. Your eleventh birthday's coming up in three weeks. Have you thought about what you want for a present?"

"Um . . ." Derek froze. He'd forgotten all about his birth-day! Normally he would have rattled off six or seven things he wanted. But just now he couldn't think of a single thing.

"Maybe a party at the batting cages for you and your friends?" his dad suggested.

"The ones *on my team*," Derek said. "The ones we're playing *against* don't need any extra help!"

"So, that's it?" his mom asked. "Nothing else?"

"Umm . . . can I think about it?"

"Sure, but don't take too long, old man. Your dad and I both have a busy week ahead. We can't be doing a lot of last-minute shopping or planning."

Suddenly it came to him. "You know what I'd *really* like? It's not actually a thing, so you wouldn't even have to go shopping."

"Well?" his dad said. "Come on, let's hear it."

"Do you think I could maybe . . . bring a friend with me

to Grandma and Grandpa's house this summer? I mean, just for a week or so." He flinched, expecting them to say no right off the bat.

But they didn't. "Hmm," his mom said thoughtfully. "I wonder if they'd be okay with that. What do you think, Jeter?"

"They're your folks, Dot. I guess you'd know best. Who'd you have in mind, Derek? Vijay?"

"Uhhh . . ."

The awful truth was, he hadn't even *thought* of Vijay. And why not? Vijay was his best friend just as much as Dave was.

But somehow it was Dave whom Derek had envisioned joining him in New Jersey. Derek could picture the two of them playing golf, going to the batting cages and Yankees games.

Vijay was great, sure, but Derek was way into sports, and Dave was more of a natural athlete. Derek could picture the two of them beating the local kids in half-court basketball or touch football.

"Actually, I thought I'd ask Dave, if that's okay."

"Dave? Ah, I see," said Mr. Jeter. "Well, why not? He's a good kid too. Assuming his parents give their permission, of course."

"Great! So I can bring him if Grandma and Grandpa say it's okay?"

"It can't hurt to ask them," said Mrs. Jeter. "But if they

have any hesitation at all, Derek, I'm not going to push it. They work very hard as it is, not to mention taking care of you and Sharlee the whole time. Still, it's a nice idea. I know it must be hard for you sometimes to be without all your friends the whole summer."

"It's not that," Derek said. "Grandma does lots of stuff with us. Our cousins are nearby, so we get to play with them a lot. And there are the Williams kids down the road. They're pretty cool. But there's nothing like having one of your best friends with you, you know?"

"I understand, old man," said his mom. "Let's see what Grandma and Grandpa say."

"Great! Thanks, Dad. Thanks, Mom."

"What about me?" Sharlee asked, frowning. "Don't I get a thank-you?"

Derek laughed, along with his parents. "You especially, Sharlee! Thank you soooo much!"

That night in bed Derek had trouble getting to sleep. He kept thinking about all the possibilities. There were so many things he and Dave could do in New Jersey. It was going to be the best week of the whole summer.

But he didn't want to get too far ahead of himself. First there was this Saturday to think of, when the two of them would have their first-ever overnight at Derek's.

Vijay had already come over lots of times over the past two years, but Dave never had. Derek wanted to make sure he had all his best games ready, and that the basketball was all blown up and ready for some one-on-one.

Speaking of not getting ahead of himself—before Dave even came over, there was the next playoff game to think about. Not to mention studying for finals.

How was a kid ever supposed to get to sleep?

Derek's wandering thoughts finally settled on the one thing that meant the most to him this week—game two. His dad had said he was worried about the team members keeping their focus.

Right as usual, Dad, Derek thought. The Indians had barely made it into the playoffs, after all. They certainly couldn't take anything for granted.

Lying there in the dark, Derek wondered if there was anything *he* could do to help his teammates be ready and at their best.

His dad and Coach Bradway had already scheduled a team practice for Thursday, two days before the game. But that was four days away, a long time to wait if the team wanted to stay sharp. So Derek decided he would call an informal practice on the Hill for Tuesday afternoon. That way, at least some of the Indians could stay sharp.

The idea gave Derek comfort. Finally he fell asleep, dreaming of baseball glory.

Chapter Three

TROUBLE BREWING

The warning bell rang, and the kids crowding the hallway began closing their lockers and scrambling off to their first class of the morning.

Derek and Dave lingered behind a bit, even though they both kept an eye on the wall clock—from warning bell to late bell was five minutes flat.

"Vijay's coming," Derek said. "So are Dean, Tito, and Mason. You in?"

Dave glanced up at the clock, an anxious look on his face. "Um, I don't know, Derek. I've got a lot of studying to do. I don't think I have any extra time to practice."

"Come on, man! You and me, we're always the first ones there and the last ones to leave. If you're not there, what are the other kids going to think?"

Derek was using all his best arguing points. But this time he didn't seem able to make the sale.

It wasn't at all like Dave to avoid Derek's eyes like this and make lame excuses. Studying? They'd both been studying like mad for two weeks already. Derek knew that, because they'd done a lot of their reviewing *together*.

"Plus I've got to clean my room," Dave added. Which was a totally dumb thing to say, in Derek's opinion, because Dave's room was always spotless. The Hennums had someone clean the whole house three times a week, even though Dave and Chase were the only ones living there most of the time.

Dave's parents were away more than they were around. In fact, it was only recently, since they'd come home for the summer, that Dave seemed to have so little extra time. Derek wondered what was up with that—but only for a second.

"We'd better get to class," Dave said. "We'll be late otherwise."

They were met at the stairs by Gary Parnell. "What's up, losers?" he greeted them.

"Nothing much," Derek answered. "We're having prac-tice on the Hill after school tomorrow. You in?"

"More practice?" Gary moaned. "Ugh. What for? We've already got one on Thursday. Isn't that enough torture for one week?"

"Come on, you know you love it," Derek said with a

laugh. In spite of all Gary's protests, Derek knew that he had really come to enjoy baseball—at least the actual games, if not the practices and drills.

Baseball had been good for Gary too. It had gotten him into better shape. It had even improved his attitude, at least a little.

"I comfort myself by remembering that baseball season will soon be over," said Gary. "Order and sanity will be restored. I will have triumphed over you on every final— and you, too," he added, pointing to Dave. "And finally I will be off to math camp, my favorite event of the year."

Derek and Dave exchanged an amused glance. About Gary, at least, they could agree. He was what you'd call a character. You could never tell what he would say next, but whatever it was, it was sure to be outrageous.

"And let me remind you, Jeter, you're welcome to join me at math camp. It's not too late to sign up. It's right here in town, and it might even help you come *close* to beating me on a test or two next year." He thought for a moment, then shook his head. "Nah, on second thought, no chance. But you'd still have fun."

"I might just beat you *without* any help, just on natural talent alone." Derek glanced over at Dave to share his little joke, but Dave wasn't paying attention. He seemed lost in his own thoughts.

"Anyway, about this so-called practice," Gary said. "It's not official, right? So I don't have to come?"

"You do have to come!" Vijay said. He'd come up behind them as they'd approached the classroom door. "We are all going. Right, Derek? Right, Dave?"

Derek nodded, and so did Dave—hesitatantly.

"Well, I guess if you're all going . . . okay, maybe I'll see you there," said Gary. He opened the door, and they all filed in just as the late bell rang.

Where *was* he?

Dave had said he'd show up at practice, even if he'd only answered Vijay with a nod of his head. So what had happened since to make him change his mind?

Gary wasn't there with the rest of them either, but that didn't surprise Derek, or even bother him that much. Gary was the last kid on the team to want to get extra practice. True, he liked it when the Indians won, but his amazing laziness always took over when it came to extra exercise. Derek was sure Gary had just shrugged it off when the time had come to grab his glove, deciding to stay parked on his couch, prepping for finals.

Dave, on the other hand, *loved* baseball—almost as much as he loved golf. Derek had taught him a lot, as had Mr. Jeter and Chase. Dave was one of the best hitters on the Indians now, and definitely their best pitcher, especially since he'd added that wicked changeup Derek had taught him. The Indians counted on him more than anyone except Derek himself.

So why wasn't he there with them? If Dave had known he wasn't going to come, why had he lied about it in school the day before?

Derek felt sure that something serious was going on with his friend. Dave hadn't acted this strangely since those first days after his arrival in town, when he didn't know anybody and was sure that nobody liked him.

But that couldn't be what was going on this time, could it?

Practice wasn't going that well. Maybe the boys' minds were on their upcoming finals. But Derek thought it was more than just that.

Normally he would have been the leader, setting up drills and making sure everyone got involved and stayed focused. But today even he had trouble focusing.

In the end their practice petered out early when two of the kids decided they wanted to go home to study.

Derek wound up doing the same thing. He forced himself to concentrate on his English review, reminding himself how important good grades were to his future—and how badly he wanted to beat Gary for highest score in the class.

But all evening his thoughts kept circling back to Dave. Something serious was up with him, Derek was sure of it. And whatever it was, it was definitely nothing good.

Chapter Four

BREAKING NEWS

"Okay, I'm listening," Derek said. He and Dave were standing in front of their lockers, which stood side by side in the main hallway of Saint Augustine's school.

"My mom had the afternoon off, and she wanted to spend some time with me," Dave said. "What was I supposed to do? I've barely seen her for months, you know?"

Derek could understand Dave wanting to spend every spare minute with his parents while they were home. But then, why had Dave felt the need to come up with all those lame excuses when Derek had first told him about the practice on the Hill?

"Okay." Derek shrugged. "I guess that's a good reason. But it wasn't the same without you, man. Not nearly."

"Sorry," Dave said. "Anyhow, I'll be there for the team practice tomorrow for sure. My folks have a function in Detroit all day. Some business thing or other, I guess."

Derek noticed that Dave was looking everywhere but at him.

He wanted to ask Dave about Saturday's overnight, just to make sure there was no problem about that. But just then Gary Parnell trudged up behind them and stopped at his locker across the hall.

"And what's *your* excuse for not showing up yesterday?" Derek asked, his hurt feelings coming out in the harsh tone of his voice.

"Ugh," Gary muttered, dropping his book bag to the floor as if it were a sack of cement. "Don't even go there, Jeter. I had a very, *very* bad day yesterday."

"Why? What happened?" Derek was sorry now that he'd come on so strong.

"Get this—my mom decided that a whole season of baseball wasn't enough punishment. So she enrolled me in *karate* class, of all things! She insisted on dragging me down there after school to sign up."

"Hey, that's not so bad," Derek said, relieved it wasn't something really terrible. "Baseball season's almost over anyway, and it's always good to get exercise. You're in much better shape now than when you first joined the team."

"Thanks a lot," Gary said sarcastically. "Yeah, it's just

great. Breaking boards with my forehead. I'm sure it does wonders for the developing brain."

"Hey, you learned to like baseball, even though you started out hating it."

"Tolerate, Jeter. I came to *tolerate* it over time. But trust me, there is nothing to like about yelling 'kee-yah' and breaking your hand on a concrete block."

Derek had to laugh. Even Dave cracked a smile. "Your mom is right, Gar," Derek said. "She knows what she's talking about. So just go to karate and give it a chance. Keep telling yourself, 'Life isn't always fair.' And when it isn't, you just have to make the best of it."

Derek had no idea how that thought had gotten into his head. He supposed he'd heard it somewhere, from one or both of his parents, probably. But it seemed the right thing to say to Gary, because with an attitude like his, what else *could* you say?

Funny, though, Derek thought as they all headed for class. *First Sharlee, now Gary. Everybody wants to be Bruce Lee.*

It was late in the evening, but Derek was still studying. He thought again about Sharlee, sleeping so soundly and innocently in her bed. Wait till her teachers started piling on the homework and tests. It was so unfair, he thought. Bigger kids had so many other things to do.

There came a soft knocking on his door. "Hey, old man." His mom peeked in. "You still working?"

"Uh-huh," Derek said glumly. "Got two more chapters to go over still."

"Okay, well, here's some good news that'll make it go easier. I just got off the phone with Grandma and Grandpa, and they said it was okay for you to bring a friend for a week. So it looks like you got your big birthday wish!"

"Wow! Really? That's amazing!" Derek said, genuinely happy. He'd just been thinking about how unfair life was, and now he'd completely changed his mind. Life was *good*—no, it was *fantastic*!

"Thanks, Mom," he said, hugging her. "That's the best news ever!"

"Don't thank me. Thank your grandparents. You can write them a nice letter tomorrow."

"Sure thing. Wow. Incredible!"

"Well, I'll let you get back to work," she said, and disappeared into the hallway.

Derek went back to his studying, but he found it harder to concentrate now. His mind kept returning to the prospect of having fun with Dave in Jersey. And the more he tried to imagine telling Dave the good news, the more he remembered how strangely Dave had been acting all week.

What if Dave doesn't even want to come? Derek had to ask himself. After all, Dave hadn't seemed too keen about their upcoming overnight, or practicing on the Hill, or even just hanging out.

So now the question was, should Derek even mention the big news to Dave?

"Attaboy, Mason! Way to get that ball back in!" Coach Jeter yelled, clapping his hands. "Lookin' good out there! Lookin' good!"

Derek agreed. He had not seen the Indians look this sharp since their run of victories back in May. It was a good feeling to know they hadn't lost their mojo. The difference between this practice and the one he'd tried to organize on the Hill was enormous.

Even Dave, who was still acting weird toward Derek at school, seemed more like his usual self here on the field. He and Derek gave each other high fives whenever either of them made a good play in the infield or made a great pitch. (Dave was the team's main pitcher, but Derek or Jonathan sometimes had to fill in.)

The Indians might not have been the most talented team in the playoffs, but Derek's dad and Coach Bradway had done a great job bringing out the best in their players and getting them to play as a team. Even Gary had gone from someone who disrupted practice and distracted teammates to a player they all counted on in big moments of big games.

Derek had total confidence that the Indians were going to win the Kalamazoo Trophy in the end. When it came to the pressure of high-stakes playoff games, there was nothing like superior coaching to get your team over the top.

Whatever doubts Derek had had at Tuesday's practice were gone now. If the team played like this on Saturday—or any other day—they had every chance of winning.

In fact, Derek was feeling so good that just as practice was ending he mentioned their upcoming overnight to Dave. "So are we good to go?"

Dave pretended not to hear. Looking out at the field, he called out, "Hey, anybody see my good bat?" When nobody answered, he said, "I've got to go look for it."

"But are we confirmed?" Derek pressed him.

"Uh . . . yeah, pretty much . . ."

"Great!" Derek put up his hand for a high five. But Dave was already moving away, looking for his bat—or pretending to.

Derek looked down at the team's equipment bag and saw that the bat Dave was supposedly looking for was lying right on top, in plain sight. Derek glanced over at Coach Bradway, who was watching Dave. Derek could see that Chase seemed troubled too, and wondered if there was a connection.

Derek decided not to mention anything about the summer just yet. After all, he could always tell Dave when they had their overnight. At least Dave had already confirmed that much.

"Yeah, I'll just tell him then," Derek said to himself. "It'll be a cool surprise, for sure."

But even as he uttered the words, he wondered how Dave would respond to the news. Derek felt his stomach tighten. It let out a low growl, as if it were talking to him, saying: *Something is wrong here.*

Chapter Five

STORM CLOUDS

"So what is the product?"

"Um, 35,840 is what I get."

"Congratulations, Derek, that is correct." Vijay gave his friend a smile and a high five. The two boys were spending the evening at the Patels', doing practice worksheets for math class in preparation for their final the following Friday.

"Next example: 443 times 342."

Derek heaved a sigh, wrote the numbers down, and began calculating. Studying for math was usually not so hard for him, but right now he was having a hard time concentrating. "Umm . . . let's see . . ."

Now it was Vijay's turn to sigh. "Come on, Derek. You

know this stuff. Why is it taking you so long to come up with the answers? Is there something wrong?"

Derek looked up, startled. "No, Vij. Why do you say that?"

"You're not usually so quiet. More of a chatterbox, really. What's up with you tonight?"

Derek didn't want to share his reasons for being so quiet and distracted. It was embarrassing enough to admit that he was thinking about Dave and their plans together. What was *really* embarrassing was that he hadn't thought to include Vijay—the guy who, until Dave had come around, had been Derek's best friend.

Now Derek's *new* "best friend" seemed like he didn't even want to hang out with him, let alone visit for a week in New Jersey.

"I don't think I'm a chatterbox, exactly," Derek said, trying to change the subject.

"Oh, no? The only person who does more talking than you is me!"

Derek cracked up in spite of himself. Good old Vijay, always the most cheerful, optimistic kid around. Now *there* was a friend you could really count on, Derek thought, which made him feel even worse about not including Vijay.

Derek didn't say anything about that, though. After all, what was he supposed to say? That he was going to invite Dave to New Jersey and not ask Vijay?

Derek wished now that he'd asked permission for two

friends to come. But he hadn't. And it was probably too late now.

"Let's call it a night, huh?" Derek said. "I don't know about you, Vij, but I've got math problems coming out of my ears. I'm going to go home and do some more English review instead."

"Something is definitely up with you," Vijay said confidently. "If you are sick, you'd better go home and lie down. You don't want to miss the big game tomorrow."

"Sorry, man. I'll be fine tomorrow, don't worry."

"No need to apologize. If you're sick, I don't want to catch it, do I? Go home and rest yourself. Go!"

Derek laughed as Vijay pretended to push him out the door. "See you at ten a.m.," Vijay said.

After he got home, Derek's mood took a dive. Of course he wasn't sick. There was no danger of his missing tomorrow's game. But he hadn't been a very good best friend to Vijay, had he?

And beyond that, was it even possible to have two best friends at the same time?

"Ohhh, my aching *everything*!" Gary limped over to the Indians' bench and dropped his mitt onto the ground as if it weighed a ton. "Coach, can I please sit this game out?"

Derek knew Gary was saying it just for effect, because both coaches were out on the field, warming up their players before the game started; they couldn't hear him.

Derek was on the bench, tightening his shoelaces, so only he was able to catch Gary's act firsthand.

"What's your problem, Gar?"

"Karate class." Gary plunked himself down beside Derek. "OWW. That hurts. *Everything* hurts."

"Hey, it's good pain," Derek said encouragingly. "You're using muscles you never used before."

"Yeah. Like my arms, my legs, and my back. Argggh. I hate karate! I knew I would hate it. I hate it even more than *baseball*!"

"Hey! Come on, Gar, you don't mean that. Listen, why don't you get up and do some stretches, so you can loosen up those muscles. We need you out there today."

"If we need me, we're in big trouble. And forget about stretching. No way. It's way too hot, and I'm way too sore. I am not doing anything that requires effort.

"Come on, man . . ."

"At least not until Coach puts me into the game, which hopefully will be never."

"Okay, okay." Derek decided to give up for now. He had no strength or patience today for Gary's dramatics. Derek had other things on his mind, like the game, which would be starting in about ten minutes.

And like Dave. Derek's friend had arrived at the field with Coach Bradway, in the big Mercedes sedan that was always kept perfectly shined and polished, even when it was carrying a load of baseball equipment in the trunk.

Dave had greeted Derek and quickly jogged out to the mound to warm up. Derek had stood staring after him for a moment. Here it was, the day of their overnight, and Dave hadn't said a single word about it when he'd said hi. Was Dave so focused on the game that he didn't want to talk about anything else?

As game time drew near and the fans gathered in the stands, Dave finished warming up and came back to sit on the bench with the rest of the team. Derek noticed that Dave's parents were nowhere to be seen. That surprised him. They'd made such a fuss about spending every spare minute with their son.

Oh well. Derek guessed they didn't exactly love baseball. It had taken Dave a while to come around as well.

While Dave was clearly focused on the game, Derek was having trouble concentrating.

Dave hadn't said he *wasn't* coming, had he? In fact, he'd sort of said that everything would be cool. He just hadn't *confirmed* it.

Instead of giving in to his fears and asking about tonight, Derek decided to keep things on a positive note and to tell Dave his good news about the summer.

"Guess what? My folks and grandparents said it would be okay if you came with me to New Jersey for a whole week!" he said. "So, do you think you might be able to come?"

Dave's jaw dropped. "Oh! Oh . . . wow," he said. "That's . . . that's really . . . that's cool."

"I know, it's amazing, right? We can play baseball with my cousins, and go to Yankee Stadium and stuff." He tried to read Dave's face. But Dave seemed to be deliberately trying to hide his reaction.

"We could even maybe ask my grandma to take us to a driving range so we can hit some golf balls," Derek added, knowing how much Dave loved playing golf. "So . . . do you think your parents would be okay with it?"

"Huh?"

"You know—do you think they'd let you come?"

"Umm, I don't know . . ." Dave still seemed to be holding something back.

Finally Derek's sense of dread got the better of him. He had to know about tonight—he just had to. "Hey, is your overnight stuff in the car?" he asked, trying to sound casual.

"Um, listen, Derek . . ." Dave's face took on a pained look. "I'm not going to be able to come over tonight after all."

"*What?* But I thought you said—"

"I know. It's . . . Well, something just came up, and . . . I *can't*, that's all. I can't explain it, okay?"

"What do you mean, you can't explain?" Derek erupted. "*Why* can't you explain? You said you were coming, and not to worry about it, that it would all be cool. What happened?"

"Quit bugging me about it, okay?" Dave said, annoyed now. "Can't we just play the game and talk about it later?"

Derek stood there, stunned. The rest of the players had already gathered for their pregame cheer. Whatever else Dave had said, he was right about one thing—they had to focus on the game. Because if they didn't, today might be the end of their playoff run, and their championship hopes.

Other things—such as friendship—would have to wait for later.

Chapter Six

BATTLEGROUND

"We're going to start off with Dave on the mound," said Coach Jeter, who then proceeded to announce the batting order and positions on the field.

Derek barely listened. He heard only that he would be hitting third and playing shortstop. But beyond that he had trouble paying attention. He couldn't stop thinking about what Dave had just said.

"Okay? Let's go, team!" yelled Coach Bradway, who was always the Indians' biggest cheerleader. The Indians responded with a chorus of yells and whoops. Then they stood against the protective chain-link fence and shouted encouragement as Mason stepped to the plate to start the game.

Derek glanced over at Dave, who was staring at the action without seeming to take much of it in. He looked even more upset than Derek felt.

A loud cheer from his teammates brought Derek's attention back to the game. Mason had hit a dribbler to the first-base side of the mound and was racing up the base line to try to beat the throw. It came in just an instant too late, and the umpire yelled, "Safe!"

"Woo-hoo!" Derek shouted along with the rest of them. He clapped his hands, got his bat, and went to the on-deck circle as Dean came up to bat.

The first pitch was in the dirt, and Mason, seeing it get away from the catcher, scooted over to second. But it didn't wind up mattering, because Dean waited out a walk, letting a 3–2 fastball go by, and getting lucky when the umpire ruled it ball four.

Derek took a few final practice swings before stepping into the box. His first at bat, and already he had the chance to do some damage.

He let the first three pitches go by, just to get a good look at the Giants' pitcher's stuff. That brought the count to 2–1.

The next pitch was inside, for ball three. Derek nodded in satisfaction. The last thing the pitcher wanted to do was load the bases with nobody out. So he was bound to throw one right down the middle now.

Derek leaned back on his right foot, preparing to give

the ball a mighty clout. The pitch was right there for him, just as he'd expected. But the pitcher had been clever. He'd taken some speed off the ball, and Derek was way out in front. He grounded it straight to the shortstop, who turned it into an easy double play, the throw just beating Derek to first base.

Mason went to third on the play, but now it was all up to Dave, who was hitting in his usual cleanup spot. Derek hoped Dave would get a hit so that everyone could forget the double play Derek had just hit into.

But Dave struck out, hacking wildly at three pitches that weren't even close to being strikes. The Indians' sure-fire first-inning rally was over—with zero runs scored!

Derek slumped in disappointment, and he wasn't the only one. Both he and Dave had looked bad up there, trying to swing for the fences when all the team had needed was a simple base hit. Now the Indians would have to start another rally from scratch.

"Come on, let's go!" Coach Bradway yelled, clapping his hands. "We'll get 'em next inning. Let's get out there and defend now! Keep your heads up, guys! Stay positive!"

Derek assumed Chase was talking about him and Dave. But he just didn't seem to be able to get his mind off his troubles and back into the moment.

Dave quickly showed signs of the same problem. He couldn't get the ball over the plate, going to 3–1 on the leadoff guy before giving up a sharp line drive to center.

Luckily, Dean happened to be positioned right where the ball ended up. He barely needed to move before snagging it, and he winced as he caught the screamer with both hands, yelling, "Oww!"

That hard line drive seemed to unnerve Dave even more. He walked the next hitter, and the one after that. "Come on, Dave. Get it over!" Chase called out. "Don't worry about the batter. Just get the ball over the plate!"

Dave nodded without looking toward the bench. He made sure to throw the next pitch right over the plate.

The cleanup man swung hard and hit another line drive. It nearly knocked Tito's glove right off his hand at first base. But he made the catch—and with the runner caught off the bag, Tito stepped on first for the double play to end the inning.

The Giants had failed to score, just as the Indians had in their half of the first. In the second inning both teams went down one, two, three. Then, in the third Gary led off and hit a 2–1 pitch so hard that it caught the center fielder flat-footed and sailed right over his head.

Gary was as slow as a turtle at the best of times. Today, with his whole body sore and achy, he was a total slug. Even so, the ball was hit so far that he rounded the bases and scored easily for a home run!

"Holy mackerel!" Derek yelled as he high-fived Gary. "I can't believe you, man. I thought you didn't even want to play today!"

"I still *don't*," Gary said as he accepted back slaps and high fives from everyone on the team. "I just decided I was so upset about karate that I had to hit something really hard."

Derek laughed and shook his head. "You're unbelievable. Just keep that up the rest of the game, okay?"

It was enough to get Derek's mind off his other troubles, at least for the moment. It didn't hurt that Vijay followed Gary's homer with a walk, and then Mason tripled to score him.

When the Giants' pitcher, rattled by the sudden turn of events, threw one into the dirt that got past the catcher, Mason scampered home for a 3–0 Indians lead. Dean then struck out, and Derek came to the plate with one out and nobody on.

He told himself to be patient, but after the pitcher threw two straight strikes right by him, he had no choice but to protect the plate and swing at anything close. He wound up fouling five pitches off on the way to a well-earned walk.

"Great at bat, Derek!" Chase called out to him, clapping. "That's keeping your head in the game!"

Derek nodded slightly, to let Chase know he'd heard. "Let's go, Dave!" he yelled, clapping his hands. "Keep it going!"

His words seemed to distract Dave. He looked upset, and proceeded to ground into an easy double play, ending the inning and the Indians' rally.

Still, they had the lead now. It held up too—until the bottom of the fourth, when the Giants finally broke through, scoring two runs on four straight hits.

Dave's usual good control had seemed to desert him today, especially this inning. So it was no surprise when Derek's dad came out to the mound and tried to calm Dave down.

Derek felt his stomach do a nervous flip. If they couldn't stop this runaway Giants rally, they could easily lose this game. And in the end that might cost them a chance at making it to the championship.

Still, even when he was tired, Dave was the team's best pitcher—and Coach Jeter's visit seemed to have a good effect. Dave managed to strike out the next two batters, then get a ground ball to first to end the inning. Derek saw Dave wiping the sweat off his dripping brow as he headed for the bench. Clearly he was as relieved as Derek was.

Derek silently swore to trust in his coaches for the rest of the playoffs and to stay strong in his belief in the team. His confidence seemed to pay off in the top of the fifth, when Dean hit a two-run homer, putting the Indians up by three runs.

Even though Derek then struck out on three pitches to end the top of the inning, he felt good about the Indians' chances with just one and a half innings left to play.

His faith in the team felt justified again when Jonathan, the relief pitcher for Dave, set the Giants down in order in the fifth. And his faith stayed strong, even when the Indians went down without scoring in their half of the sixth.

It was the Giants' last licks now. Jonathan got the first hitter to pop out to Mason at second. Things were looking good, Derek thought, bouncing up and down on the balls of his feet and pounding his glove in readiness.

But then came two sharp singles on two straight pitches, resulting in two men on base and the tying run coming to the plate!

Was Jonathan getting tired already?

CRACK! It was a sizzling grounder, hit right between Derek and Dave. Derek went for it, assuming Dave was covering third—but he *wasn't*. At the last instant Derek caught sight of him coming for the ball, and he backed off, thinking Dave was going to get it.

But no. Dave backed off too. The ball skittered right between them, untouched, and rolled straight into the outfield. One run came in to score, and now there were Giants runners at first and third!

"Let's go! Let's *go!*" Coach Jeter clapped his hands together so hard that Derek thought he might hurt himself. "Heads in the game, Indians!"

Meaning him and Dave. Again.

Derek snuck a quick look at his friend and saw that Dave was near tears, staring at the dirt between his feet. "Come on, Dave!" Derek told him. "Let's get this game in the bag. Never mind anything else!"

Dave nodded without looking at Derek. He pounded his glove and stared in at the plate, ready. Derek did the same.

Jonathan's next pitch bounced off the end of Paul's catcher's mitt. The runner at third broke for home, and all Derek could do was watch as another run scored, thanks to his and Dave's misplay. Now the Indians' lead was down to one measly run.

The runner had advanced from first to second on the play and was now in position to score the tying run on a base hit—and still only one out! Could the Indians hold on to win?

Jonathan looked scared out there. Not that Derek wasn't, but he wasn't pitching. The Giants' cleanup hitter stood in the batter's box, waving his bat like a magic wand. Derek swallowed hard, remembered something his dad had once told him: "Don't be afraid to fail. If you're afraid to fail, you won't allow yourself the opportunity to succeed."

"Time-out!" Derek called out suddenly, raising his arms over his head. When the umpire granted it, Derek trotted over to the mound to talk to Jonathan.

"Don't be afraid of this guy," Derek told him. "You aren't able to play your best when you're scared. Besides, he's the one who should be scared of *you*. And you know what else?" he added with a sly grin. "He's got his pants on backward."

It wasn't true, of course. But it got a smile—even a little

laugh—out of Jonathan. And as Derek well knew, you can't laugh when you're scared—not a *real* laugh, at least.

Derek could see his dad now, standing next to Coach Bradway, staring out at the mound. They must have wondered why he'd called the time-out, and what he was saying, but they must have decided to trust him on it, because neither of them chose to join him out there.

Derek went back to his position, and the game resumed. Jonathan settled in and threw the first pitch, down and in. The hitter skipped rope, yelping, though the ball hadn't really been close to hitting his feet.

Now who's scared? Derek said to himself.

The next pitch was high and away, and the hitter flailed at it weakly. A fastball over the inside half of the plate froze him for another strike. Then, with a 1–2 count, Jonathan quickly finished him off with a curveball. The hitter swung and missed by six inches, then slammed his bat onto the plate in frustration.

The Giants and their fans called out in desperation for their team to rally, facing their final out of the game. Derek leaned forward, in the ready position. He'd already made a lot of mistakes this game, and so had Dave. He only hoped they didn't cost the Indians the game—and their chance to be champions.

Jonathan gritted his teeth and stared in at the catcher.

"Go right at him!" Derek called out. "He can't hit you, Johnny!" He knew it wasn't true, of course. But that didn't matter. What counted was Jonathan having enough confidence to throw his pitch, his way.

And he did. It was a slow curve, and the hitter whaled at it but only tapped it weakly back to the mound. Jonathan grabbed it and spun around to throw to first.

It was an easy play, and it *would* have sealed the Indians' victory—except that Jonathan slipped as he turned, and his throw sailed high and wide of the bag!

Tito leapt for it, but he couldn't snag it. The ball skittered away, and the runner at second, who'd already passed third base, came around to score, while the hitter reached second base on the error.

Derek let out a groan, echoed by every Indians player and fan. Now the game was tied. They'd let their lead slip away, and with one more measly little hit, the Giants would steal the victory that should have been theirs.

Derek had to fight back tears. If only Jonathan hadn't slipped. If only he and Dave hadn't messed up earlier in the inning. He was furious at himself for getting distracted and letting that happen.

It had been partly Dave's fault too, of course, but that was just the point. Whatever was going on between them, they shouldn't have let it affect their play. This game was way too important.

Derek felt the sick feeling returning to the pit of his stomach as Jonathan fell behind the next batter, 2–0. On the third pitch Jonathan threw a fastball right over the middle of the plate, and the hitter smashed a screaming line drive to Gary's left.

A faster fielder might have reached it and caught it with a dive. But Gary had never dived for a ball—or for anything else, for that matter. The ball skittered right by him, and the Giants' runner came home to score the winning run.

"NOOOO!" Derek yowled as he watched the disaster unfold.

The Giants all threw their mitts and caps into the air and jumped skyward after them. They swarmed the guy who'd gotten the winning hit, jumping up and down.

Derek caught just a glimpse of the celebration, then turned away. It was painful to watch, and even more painful to think how it could have been *them* celebrating—and how they'd blown it.

As the Indians made their way to the bench and started packing up their gear, their coaches had a few choice words for the players.

"Keep your chins up, boys," said Chase. "Listen up now. We beat ourselves today, Indians. We were far from playing our best, the way we did at practice last Thursday. I think we all agree there's lots of room for improvement— and that goes for every one of us. Coach Jeter?"

"We're not out of this thing yet—not by a long shot," Derek's dad told the team. "We're 1–1. If we win next week, we can still make it into the finals. So this is no time to get down on ourselves. All we have to do is bring our A game next week and leave any distractions behind.

"Now go home, all of you, and think about how *you* can do better next time. We'll see you at practice next Thursday. We're going to spend the whole time on two things—fundamentals and playing together as a team."

Neither coach had named names, but Derek knew whom Coach Bradway had meant when he'd said the team hadn't played its best. He and Dave had made most of the mistakes out there today. And Derek knew why too.

In the car afterward, nobody said much. Not until Derek and his dad had dropped Vijay off at the other end of Mount Royal and were driving back to the parking lot in front of their apartment.

"It's so *unfair!*" Derek suddenly blurted out. "We had that game won, even after Dave and I blew that play. If only Jonathan hadn't slipped on that play, we still would've won!"

"I know it *seems* unfair," his dad said, turning off the engine but making no move to open the car door. "We got a few bad breaks today. But if you remember back a week, we were lucky to win that one. I'll bet there are lots of kids on the Dodgers who think it wasn't fair that they lost to us."

Derek remembered the faces of that defeated team, their stunned expressions. He guessed what his dad was saying was true.

"Next week maybe the breaks will go our way again," Derek's dad said. "These things tend to even out over time. But in the end, Derek, we can't control the breaks. We can't control what anybody else does. We can only control our own selves, our own actions. It's best to pay attention to that and ignore all the stuff we can't control."

"I guess," said Derek. Not that it made him feel any better. A loss was a loss. But this loss, he knew, was partly his own fault.

"All right, Derek. You want to tell me what was going on with you out there today?"

Did he *want* to? Of course not. But Derek knew there was no sense in keeping anything from his dad—or his mom, for that matter—and no way to hide it either. After all, they were the ones who were supposed to be in charge of Derek and Dave's overnight tonight.

Derek heaved a sigh and said, "Dave isn't staying over at our house tonight. I have no idea why, and he won't tell me. Oh, and I asked him about this summer? He seemed kind of so-so about that, too. So I guess I can forget about him coming to New Jersey. If he won't even be straight with me about tonight, he's never going to come for a *week*."

His dad stayed quiet, for what seemed to Derek like a long time. Finally he said, "Wow. That hurts." He nodded slowly, taking it all in. "I'm so sorry, Derek."

Derek nodded, glad that his dad understood.

"You know what, though? I'm sure there's a very good reason why Dave's not coming. I'm also sure there's a very good reason why he feels he can't tell you about it. Maybe in time he will."

Derek wasn't at all sure about that. In fact, Dave's body language and his lame excuses told Derek just the opposite.

"Maybe you could try asking him about rescheduling for next Saturday," Mr. Jeter suggested. "I'd be okay with that, and I'm pretty sure your mom would be too."

"What's the point?" Derek said, still feeling defeated.

"I'll tell you what—there's *no* point in sweating it right now. You've got finals to think about, not to mention the team. I understand what happened on that field now, but you've got to move on and go forward. We all do."

With that, he got out of the car. Derek sat in the passenger seat long after his dad had disappeared into the house.

This coming Monday he would be taking the first of his finals. Between now and then he had to spend most of his time studying, because there was a lot of stuff they'd covered during the year, and he needed to go over it all at least once. Derek wanted to do his best, for sure—and he wanted even more to beat Gary for best grade in the class!

But Derek knew his dad was right. If he didn't get things straightened out with Dave by next Saturday, he might not be able to concentrate enough to play his best.

So he decided right there and then that the first chance he got, he would ask Dave about next Saturday night. If Dave said yes, great. If he said no, and still refused to explain, that would mean he really didn't want to be Derek's friend anymore.

Either way, at least Derek would know for sure.

Chapter Seven

TRICKS AND TESTS

"*Keeee-yah!* Now watch this one! *Keeee-yah!*"

Dessert must have gotten Sharlee going, because now she was a bundle of energy and excitement. Her "demonstration" of what she'd learned in karate class had the whole family clapping and laughing.

Even Derek, who was thrilled to get his mind off his own troubles for a while—not to mention the three hours he'd just spent studying—joined in the fun.

"Stop laughing!" Sharlee demanded, annoyed. "It's not funny!"

"We're not laughing *at* you, honey," Mrs. Jeter said. "We're laughing *with* you, because you're so amazing. For someone who just started karate, you've got a fantastic kick there!"

"Kee-*yah*! Kee-*yah*! *Hah!*" Sharlee launched kicks and punches into the air, so fast that their dad had to give her an affectionate bear hug to make sure she didn't get out of control and hurt herself or break something. The living room was big, and the furniture was all pulled out of the way, but still . . .

"You are fantastic, Sharlee!" Mr. Jeter said as he held her up over his head.

"Stop it, Daddy," she complained, giggling in spite of herself. "I'm still mad!"

"Don't be mad, Sis," said Derek. "Hey, let's see if you can flip me!"

"*Derek*," Mrs. Jeter warned softly, "it's almost bedtime. Sharlee's tired—"

"I'm *not* tired!" said Sharlee, who always seemed to have superhuman hearing. "Come on, Derek. I'm ready! Are *you* ready?"

"Hmm. Maybe just for a minute." Mrs. Jeter rolled her eyes and shook her head, accepting the inevitable.

"I want to see this," Mr. Jeter said with a shrug. "I guess you kids can give it a try. Once. And stay away from the furniture."

"Okay. Pretend I'm coming at you really fast, Sharlee." Derek reached his arms out toward her. "Now grab this arm and yank it down and backward."

"Like this?" Sharlee asked.

"Whoooa!" As she yanked his arm, Derek made himself

flip forward, a trick he'd learned in gym the previous fall. He rolled to a soft landing, hamming it up and making it look like she'd really flipped him.

Sharlee jumped up and down, clapping. "Yay! That was *awesome*. Let's do it again!" She knew, of course, that Derek had actually flipped himself, but that didn't bother her one bit. It was still a great trick. It had even fooled her parents! At least that was what she thought.

"Sharlee, it's bedtime now," said Mrs. Jeter.

"One more time! Pleeeease?"

"Sharlee," said Mr. Jeter sternly. "You know there's no arguing with your mother. Or with me. We said once. That means once."

And that was that. In the Jeter house, mom's or dad's word was law. Derek watched Sharlee go slowly up the stairs, acting like a very sad little girl. Then she looked back over her shoulder and grinned at Derek mischievously. With a little giggle she disappeared around the landing.

Derek was still laughing, but he had no doubt that one day soon enough Sharlee really would be able to flip him.

Derek was always happy when he was making his sister happy. But that night, lying in bed, the grim reality began to sink back in.

What could possibly have changed things so much between him and Dave? Two weeks ago they'd been best buds—on the same team, in the same class, hanging out all the time. What had happened to all that?

The answer seemed to flash in front of his eyes. Dave's parents had arrived two weeks ago. And nothing had been the same since.

Derek didn't want it to be true. He didn't want that to be the explanation. Because it would mean that Dave's parents didn't like him. And that would be *awful*.

Derek hated to think it was Dave's mom and dad who were keeping them from being friends. But there was the evidence to consider. Since the Hennums had come back from their travels, Derek and Dave hadn't hung out even once.

On the other hand, he thought, what if he was wrong? What if Dave's parents had no problem with him? That would be even worse. It would mean it was *Dave's* idea to back off their friendship.

More terrible possibilities flitted through Derek's mind. Had Dave's parents convinced him not to like Derek? Or was Dave being punished for being Derek's friend? Every possibility was terrible, and worst of all was not knowing what was true and what wasn't.

Derek tried to think of what it was he might have done wrong. There must have been something. There had to be a reason why Dave's parents didn't like him—*if* they didn't, that is.

No, he decided after long consideration. He hadn't done anything wrong. Nothing at all. He'd been nice, and polite, and he'd been a good friend to Dave all this time. Chase liked Derek. So why didn't they?

He might never have gotten to sleep, but his dad's words finally came back to him: "We can only control our own selves, our own actions." Derek decided to ask Dave about next Saturday—first thing Monday morning, even before the test, if possible.

Now that Derek had decided on a course of action, he promised himself he wouldn't think about it again until Monday morning.

And with that, he finally made it to dreamland.

Derek sat at his desk, his study materials for the English final laid out in front of him. But he wasn't really looking at them. In spite of himself, he kept glancing up at the door whenever it opened and another student came in.

He was waiting for Dave. He'd already determined that he was going to ask Dave about next week the minute he got the chance. He knew he should be concentrating on acing this test, but he just couldn't help it. He had to know what was going on. If he only knew the truth, he told himself, he would be able to get past it and concentrate on the final.

Gary came in, looking grim. Derek was curious. What was bothering Gary? Was it karate class? He usually came in totally psyched for tests—*especially* finals! He lived for days like this, and yet . . .

Derek was curious, but his attention turned quickly from Gary the minute Dave walked into the classroom. Dave's desk was right behind Derek's, so there was no way for Dave to avoid Derek as he passed.

"Hi!" Derek said, trying to sound as close to normal as possible.

"Oh. Hi." Dave barely looked at him as he took his seat and opened his book bag, looking for something. (A pencil? Something else? Or was he just trying to avoid eye contact?)

"Hey, Dave, you want to come over next Saturday night? My folks said it's okay."

Dave froze for a moment. Without looking up, he said, "Uh, I don't know . . . Sure, I guess . . ."

Derek felt a fresh sting of hurt. *A little enthusiasm would have been nice,* he thought. Well, at least he'd said yes. Sort of.

Looking to his left, Derek saw Vijay quickly turn away. Vijay pretended to be straightening his pencils, but he had a sad look on his face.

Was he listening the whole time? Derek wondered. *Oh, great,* he thought. Derek felt like his head was about to explode. Now he had trouble with both of his best friends!

Thankfully, the bell rang and the test got under way. To his own surprise, Derek found it easy to concentrate. But that made perfect sense, of course.

He desperately wanted to think about anything other than what had just gone down.

Chapter Eight

WHAT LIES BENEATH?

Thursday's practice felt flat. Four members of the team, including Gary, hadn't shown up. There weren't even enough kids for a scrimmage. And although the Indians went through their drills well enough, there wasn't a lot of team spirit, either. It was as if the season were already over and these few kids were the only ones who didn't realize it.

Derek's dad and Coach Bradway must have sensed it too, because after practice that was the theme they harped on. "This season isn't over for us—not yet. Not by a long shot," said Chase. "We've got to keep our minds focused on our mission."

"I know you boys have finals to study for, and summer

plans you're looking forward to," said Coach Jeter. "But no matter what else is going on in your lives, when you're here at the ball field, you've got to be *here*. I'll tell you one thing, the Twins are going to show up ready to beat us on Saturday. We'd better be ready too—because if we aren't, we'll be 1–2 and our season really *will* be over."

"And that would be a shame," Coach Bradway added. "We've come a long way. Let's finish the job! Gimme an *I*!"

Chase began the team chant that spelled out "INDIANS." The team responded halfheartedly at first, but by the end, when the name got repeated three times in a row, everyone was fully into it.

"Okay, see you all at the game," said Derek's dad. "And let's show up ready to win!"

After practice Derek found Dave at the end of the bench, stuffing bats back into the team's duffel bag. "Don't forget about our overnight," he said, coming right out with it.

For three days at school neither of them had said a word to each other. Instead Derek had hung out with Vijay, who was clearly glad to have Derek's company.

But it was already Thursday now, and Derek knew it was time to break through the wall of silence Dave had put up between them.

"I can't come Saturday," Dave said, cinching up the bat bag. "Sorry."

Derek was stunned. "But . . . but why not?" he asked. "On Monday you said—"

"I just said that so you wouldn't keep pressuring me!" Dave blurted out.

"Sorry. I thought we were friends."

"We *are* friends."

"Then why don't you want to come over?"

"I do! I just—I *can't*, that's all."

"Why not? If we're friends, you can at least tell me that."

"No. I can't," said Dave, almost choking up.

"Man, you're different from how you used to be." Derek shook his head. "I don't know what I did wrong, but—"

"It's nothing you did."

"Then what is it?"

Dave sighed deeply. "My parents just want to have some time with me, that's all. They didn't see me all these months, so . . ."

Maybe Derek had been blowing this whole thing out of proportion. "You know, you could have just *told* me that in the first place," he said. "I would have understood. Or at least tried to."

"Sorry. But you can see why now, right?"

"Not totally. I mean, that explains some things but not everything. Like why you never come out to the Hill anymore. Or why you haven't been able to look me in the eye for the past two weeks."

"I *do* look you in the eye! And I'm not hiding anything!" Well, at least he was looking at Derek now. "Just quit pestering me about everything, will you? When I can hang out again, I will. Okay?" So saying, he grabbed the bat bag and marched off toward the big Mercedes, where Chase was waiting to drive him home.

Derek stared after him, even more troubled than he'd been before. He wondered if Dave had told him the whole truth—or maybe Dave hadn't been telling any of the truth even now. Derek felt sure his friend was still hiding something.

"Mom?"

"Yes, Derek? Something on your mind?"

The room was dark except for the night-light plugged into the wall. Derek's mom sat on the side of his bed. She'd just kissed him good night and had been about to leave, when he'd stopped her. "Mom . . . did Dad tell you anything about Dave?"

"Well, he did say something. . . ."

"What did he say?"

"Only that he thought something was upsetting your friendship. And of course, Dave did cancel the overnight, but he's coming this Saturday, isn't he?"

Derek sighed. "No."

"But didn't you say—"

"That was *then*. Today he said he couldn't. He said his parents want to spend more time with him."

"Well, there's nothing wrong with that."

"But I don't think that's the real reason, Mom. If they wanted to spend time with Dave so much, how come they spent so many months away from home?"

"Well, they *had* to. For business. Grown-ups don't always have a choice about these things."

"They could have brought Dave with them wherever they went," Derek said. "They could have got him a tutor, just like they got Chase to take care of him here."

"Derek, family life is complicated, and different families do things different ways. All we can do is make sure our own family stays happy, healthy, and together."

"But the point is, that's not the real reason," Derek protested.

"How do you know that?"

"I don't *know* how I know. I just *do* know. Like, from the way Dave doesn't look at me when he talks. And the way he gets annoyed whenever I suggest hanging out. It's like he doesn't even *want* to. I think he's just blaming his parents because he doesn't want to admit it's him. Maybe he's just using them as an excuse for not being friends anymore."

"Oh, Derek," his mom said softly, "why wouldn't Dave want to be friends with you? He certainly did before, and *you* haven't changed, have you?"

"No," Derek had to admit. "But he sure has. And I can't figure out what it's all about. It's so unfair!"

"Derek, I understand how you must feel. It's awful, I

can see that, but all you can do is keep on being a good friend and being true to yourself."

"Yeah, yeah, I know," said Derek. "Life's not always fair. Blah, blah, blah."

"I also recommend being honest with Dave about how you're feeling. Maybe then he might be willing to talk it out with you. And if he does," she added, "be careful not to blame him—or anyone else. Just be truthful about your feelings, and then . . . sit back and *listen*."

Chapter Nine

FRIENDS AND FINALS

Derek came to school on Friday fully prepped and ready for his big math final. He felt like he'd done okay on the English final, even though they hadn't gotten their grades back yet. But math was Derek's favorite subject, and he really wanted to do well on this one, especially because math was also Gary's favorite.

Gary was sure to give him a hard time about it when he came in, just to try to psych Derek out. Gary was as competitive as Derek was. It was probably the only thing they had in common, as far as Derek could see. But it helped Derek understand Gary—sort of.

Much to Derek's surprise, though, Gary didn't say a word to anyone. He just settled slowly into his seat, looking gloomy and wincing in discomfort.

That had to be because of karate class, Derek figured. He had asked Gary about it the day before, but Gary had refused to even talk about it. In fact, he'd seemed kind of sad. And today he seemed even worse.

Boy, he must really, really hate that class, thought Derek. He sure hoped Gary would be feeling better by the time tomorrow's game rolled around!

During their last game, Gary had used his anger to hit a big home run. But honestly, a repeat performance was far from a sure thing. The rest of the team was going to have to improve, starting with Derek and Dave.

But how, if they weren't even talking to each other?

Dave arrived just as the bell rang. Ms. Fein told them to take their seats and have their pencils ready. Derek wondered if Dave had arrived at the last moment on purpose so he could avoid speaking to Derek.

Gary opened his book bag, took out some pencils, and was instantly all business. Derek knew he'd better concentrate totally on the test if he had any hope of besting Gary, who was a total brainiac and usually never stopped talking about it.

When Derek next looked up, it was half an hour later, and Gary was already handing in his paper! Everyone else in the room was still working. Derek himself was only about halfway done. *Uh-oh,* he thought. He'd been finding the test pretty hard, but for Gary it obviously had been a breeze.

Derek finished with just five minutes to spare before

the end of the test period. He looked over at Dave, who was still working, along with about ten other kids.

Derek knew his mom's advice was good. If he and Dave were going to continue to be friends, they were going to have to talk things out. But it was easier said than done. Dave wasn't exactly giving him the opening. Now their talk would probably have to wait till after tomorrow's game.

That afternoon Derek and Vijay were at the Patels' house, studying for next Wednesday's science final. Derek hadn't felt like studying alone, and Vijay was pretty smart, especially in science. Besides, he was always fun to hang out with. Being here with him felt relaxing.

There was never any doubt whether Vijay liked Derek, not like with Dave. Derek always knew he could be straight with Vijay too.

"I thought Dave was my best friend," Derek blurted out—and immediately wished he hadn't. The hurt in Vijay's expression was as plain as day. "I mean, my *other* best friend. Of course."

When Vijay still looked sad, Derek added, "You *can* have two best friends, you know." But he knew that didn't make up for the fact that until Dave had moved to town, Vijay had been Derek's only best friend.

Vijay seemed to brighten at Derek's words, at least a little. But Derek could tell he'd hurt his friend's feelings. He felt like kicking himself.

"That really stinks, doesn't it?" Vijay said. "But then again, what can you do about it? If someone stops liking you, you can't make them like you again, can you?"

Derek hoped Vijay was talking about Dave, not about Vijay and Derek. But Derek knew it was true. You couldn't force someone to be your friend.

"Hey, Vij," Derek suddenly said. "You want to come to New Jersey with me this summer for a week? I know it's expensive to fly there and back, but it would be a blast if you could."

Derek didn't know what he would do if both Vijay and Dave said yes. He hadn't asked permission to invite a second friend!

But Vijay solved the problem for him. "Unlucky for me, but still lucky—my family is going to India for the whole summer, for my cousin's wedding."

"A wedding takes all summer?"

Vijay laughed. "You don't know what Indian weddings are like! Very different from here."

Derek was sorry Vijay couldn't come. It really would have been a blast to have him there, with or without Dave. But at least this way Derek wouldn't get caught with both his friends saying yes to just one invitation.

On the other hand, now it was down to just Dave, and that didn't look like a likely prospect. It suddenly hit Derek that he might not get his birthday wish after all.

Chapter Ten

VICTORY AND DEFEAT

On Saturday morning Derek awoke with one thing on his mind—the game at eleven o'clock. Outside, dark clouds covered the sky, and when he brought the team equipment out to the car with his dad, Derek could smell rain in the air.

He sure hoped it held off till later in the day. It would be awful if the game had to be postponed! It had been hard enough to get himself psyched and ready after taking two big finals this week.

And then there was the Dave thing, of course. Derek had promised himself not to think about it till after the game, but it still got him down every time it popped into his head. *Like now.*

Luckily, Vijay came to the rescue. He was waiting outside his apartment when Derek and his dad rolled up in the old station wagon, and hopped into the backseat.

"Oh boy!" Vijay said. "We are going to have to play fast today, or we will all get wet!" He was so excited, he was almost bouncing up and down on the seat.

Derek was glad to see Vijay in a good mood again, because it meant he had forgotten about feeling like Derek's second-best friend. Derek's invitation to come to New Jersey had obviously been a stroke of inspiration—even if Vijay wasn't able to accept it.

"We are going to win, win, win!" Vijay chanted in a sing-song voice, still bouncing and swaying to his own beat. *"Yes, yes, yes. Win, win, win!"*

By now both Derek and his dad were laughing and bopping along to Vijay's crazy beat. They arrived at the field, and Mr. Jeter parked right up close. "Okay, everybody out," he said. "We've got work to do."

The boys helped him unload the wagon—batting helmets, catcher's gear, and lots of baseballs. The bats were with Coach Bradway, along with the scorebooks and other odds and ends. Derek saw the Mercedes as it parked just down the street.

Chase got out first, then Dave. But *not* Dave's parents. *Hmmm,* thought Derek. *Not here again.* He wondered what was up with that. Did they just hate baseball? Didn't they understand how much their son loved playing?

Or maybe, Derek thought with a tinge of bitterness, they were busy as usual, doing some business thing or other. He felt kind of sorry for Dave. Even though Chase was a great guy, and a kid couldn't have had a better guardian when his parents were away, it wasn't the same thing as having your own mom and dad around.

But that was just it. They *were* around now—supposedly—but where were they? Try as he might, Derek just could not make any sense of it.

Dave brought a bag full of bats over, and Chase followed with another. Some of the other team members had already arrived—Eddie, Miles, Paul, Dean—and the boys began throwing the ball around, warming up their arms.

When enough of them had arrived, Coach Bradway said, "Okay, twice around the base paths—now!" Both coaches wanted their team to be loose before the game, so that they wouldn't hurt themselves by pulling a muscle later, in the heat of action.

They had fifteen minutes to practice. Then it was the Twins' turn, and the Indians gathered back at the bench. It was time for the coaches' pregame speeches.

"Thursday's practice, as you know," said Chase, "was not very well attended. I guess some of you were busy studying for finals. At least, I hope so. Anyway, for those of you who showed, I'm sure you agree it felt a little off, a little short on team spirit.

"Well, I hope you're ready to compete today," he went

on. "Because this is the last game of the round-robin. If we win, we're into the finals. If not, we're done. It's one or the other—win or go home. So let's not leave anything to chance, huh? Let's bring our best!"

"YEAH!" all the Indians shouted together.

"Coach Jeter?"

"Thanks, Coach Bradway," said Mr. Jeter. "Boys, I just want to say before you go out there that I'm proud of each and every one of you. I'm proud of all the effort you've given this season, how much you've improved, and I'm proud to have been your coach."

The whole team was silent. Coach Jeter waited about five seconds, letting his words sink in, before he added, "Now let's make sure this *isn't* our last game, and that we get to keep playing until we've got that Kalamazoo Trophy in our hands!"

"Yeah!" some of the kids said, clapping.

"I know you've all had a lot on your minds." He gave Derek a quick glance, and Derek saw Chase look over at Dave. "But I want you to put everything else aside and focus on winning this game—one pitch, one swing, one play at a time. Now get out there and show 'em how it's done!"

"YEAH!" the whole team bellowed, raising their fists skyward. "GO, INDIANS!"

Derek felt the energy coursing through him. Dave, too, had a determined look on his face. Even Gary was pounding on his mitt, eager for the game to begin. It seemed to Derek that his dad's words had inspired the whole team. He only hoped they would carry that inspiration out onto the field.

Mason got into the batter's box, and the Indians started cheering at the tops of their lungs. Mason was small and got a lot of walks, but after two pitches he was already in the hole with two strikes.

"Hang in there, Mase!" Derek heard himself yelling. "Hang tough!"

Mason might not have heard him amid all the noise, but he did hang tough, letting an inside curveball hit him in the arm. "Ow!" he yelled, grabbing his elbow, dropping the bat, and going into a crouch. "My funny bone! OW!"

"Take your base!" the umpire said, and Mason trotted down to first, rubbing the sting from his elbow. By the time he got there, he seemed to forget he'd been hit in the arm. A broad grin replaced the grimace he'd just worn on his face.

Had he let the ball hit him on purpose? It had been a slow pitch. Maybe Mason had just been frozen by it, but it didn't seem to Derek like he'd tried very hard to get out of the way. And now, that smile . . .

"Let's go!" Derek shouted, clapping as Dean came up to bat. He took the first pitch in the dirt for a ball—and Mason scampered over to second, beating the throw by a hair!

"That-a-way!" Derek called, grabbing his bat and heading for the on-deck circle. It was so loud on the Indians' bench and in their section of the bleachers that he couldn't even hear his own voice.

Dean saw five pitches, fouling off three of them, before he laced a sharp single to right—scoring Mason from second base for the team's first run!

"Ya-hoooo!" Derek shouted. "Woo!" It was only 1–0, but the run felt bigger than that. It showed that the Indians had come to play today, and that they were determined to win—somehow, some way.

Derek walked to the plate, telling himself to keep calm, to be patient, to swing only at strikes. He let the first two pitches go by for balls.

On the second one Dean tried to steal second base. The catcher got up and fired. Dean slid to the outside of the bag and got around the second baseman's tag.

"Safe!" the umpire called.

Now Derek needed only a single to drive in the team's second run. The count was in his favor, 2–0. The pitcher came in with a fastball on the outside corner, but Derek didn't try to pull it. He just slapped it the other way.

The ball looped in the air, dropped behind the first baseman, and kept on rolling into foul territory, where the right fielder picked it up and threw to second base—too late. Derek was already there, and the Indians had scored their second run on his RBI!

"That's so unfair!" he overheard the second baseman tell the first baseman. "He hardly touched that ball!" Derek had to smile. He'd been on the other side of that one not too long ago.

Up next, Dave worked the count full, fouled off two tough pitches, and took the next pitch outside for a walk. Then everyone on the Indians let out a triumphant yell and a sigh of relief when Tito followed with a three-run blast over the right fielder's head!

It was 5–0, and still nobody out in the first inning! This game had the makings of a rout, Derek thought. He looked around at his teammates and saw that they could barely contain their excitement. Vijay was literally jumping up and down in front of the bench. Even Gary was sitting there clapping!

Although the Indians didn't score again that inning, they kept tacking on runs, one here, one there. By the sixth inning they led 8–2 and were only three outs away from a spot in the final!

But the Twins, while they hadn't scored much, had gotten their share of hits and walks, fouled off a lot off pitches, and made Dave work hard all game. He'd thrown a lot of pitches in those first five innings. In fact, he'd reached his limit according to league rules.

Derek figured that meant Jonathan would take over in relief. He was shocked when his dad signaled for *Derek* to take the ball instead!

Derek didn't *hate* pitching. But he felt most comfortable at his favorite position, shortstop. Not to mention, he hadn't pitched for the team in weeks.

Even worse, it had just started to rain. Not hard, just a little drizzle, but it was wet enough to make the ball slippery.

Derek's heart started pounding the moment he took the ball from his dad's hand. Dave went out to play third base, with Jonathan shifting to short in Derek's place. Vijay replaced Eddie in right field, and Gary took over for Jonah in left.

Derek threw a few warm-up pitches, then nodded to tell the ump he was ready. The Twins batter stepped into the box. Derek blew out a deep breath, relaxed his shoulders, and got down to business.

Maybe it was the long layoff. Maybe it was just nerves. But for some reason Derek could not seem to locate the strike zone. His arm felt fine, but his pitches were all over the place. He walked the first two batters he faced, on just ten pitches!

That brought Coach Bradway out to the mound for a talk. "Just throw strikes," he said.

Derek nodded, even though it was obvious that if he could have thrown strikes, he would have.

"Play catch with Miles, that's all. Put it right into his glove. Don't be afraid of these guys." Chase gave him a pat on the back and returned to the bench.

Somehow the short break, or Chase's words, must have helped, because Derek quickly threw two strikes past the hitter. But on his next pitch—another one right down the middle—the batter mashed the ball for what looked like a hundred miles.

The two men on base, and the slugger himself, practically walked around the bases. Vijay quickly gave up on chasing the ball, which had disappeared into the woods at the end of Westwood Fields and was gone forever. The umpire fished out a brand-new baseball to replace it.

Now it was 8–5, Indians, and *it was all Derek's fault*! They'd had a safe lead, and now he'd gone and given it up, letting the Twins right back into the game.

He could sense the worry of the players behind him and the Indians fans in the stands. He could feel the growing excitement of the Twins fans as they cheered their team on.

Now that he'd been hit hard, Derek found he was once again having trouble throwing strikes. This time it really was out of fear—fear of a batter shellacking it for another homer!

His dad and Chase might have been the best coaches in the world, but in the end it was the players who had to go out there and win or lose. Was he about to lose this game and end the entire season for his team?

Two walks later his dad came slowly out to the mound and mercifully took the ball from him. "Go on out to center," he told Derek as he motioned for Jonathan to take over on the mound, Mason to move to short, and Eddie to play second.

"Center?"

His dad nodded. Downcast, Derek jogged slowly to the outfield. Dean patted him on the back with his glove as he passed, saying, "Don't worry, man. We're gonna pick you up. We're going to win this game. You'll see."

Derek suddenly found himself fighting back tears. It was all so unfair! Why did he have to go and choke at the worst possible moment?

Then he remembered what his dad and Chase had said, about keeping your head in the game. He shook himself off, trying to shake the blues away and focus on this critical moment.

He forced his attention back to the game, and not a second too soon. On Jonathan's first pitch the batter smacked one right in Derek's direction.

Sensing that the ball would have a lot of carry, Derek started running back immediately. Even so, he had to make a flying leap to snag it—and he barely held on as he crashed to the ground and slid for several feet on the wet grass. But he held the ball! And that made one out. Two more to go!

Both runners had tagged up on the play and then moved to second and third. But at least no one had scored—for the moment.

Jonathan must not have had his best stuff today, because the next batter hit it hard too, right up the middle. Derek charged it, knowing he couldn't catch it on the fly and that it was going to drop in for a hit.

The man on third would score for sure, but Derek thought that if he got to it quickly and threw home, he might just nail the second runner at the plate—if he didn't slip and fall trying, that is.

He fielded it cleanly and threw it as hard as he could, launching himself clear off the ground. The ball got there a second before the runner, and Miles tagged him out, saving a run and leaving the score at 8–6.

On the throw the hitter had advanced to second base. He was now in scoring position, but even if he made it home, it wouldn't tie the game. That two-run cushion gave Derek at least a little comfort. But not for long.

The next hitter lined a hard shot to left. It landed in front of Gary, who saw that he couldn't stop the runner from scoring. So he threw to second base, trying to keep the hitter at first.

But the ball must have hit a rock, because it took a bad hop, eluding the second baseman and allowing the runner to get all the way to third.

Now the Twins were only one hit away from tying the game! The rain was coming down harder and harder, but since it was the last inning, Derek felt sure the umps would let them finish—if they could get the last out quickly enough, that is.

Jonathan was getting shelled. Derek could tell he was

scared, but Derek was too far away to give his pitcher any encouragement. Why had Derek's dad put him out here in center field, anyway? Why couldn't his dad just have let him play short?

He forced his attention back to the game again. This moment was too important for him to let himself get distracted. Besides, he'd already cost his team a bunch of runs. He didn't want to be the one who lost the game for them in the end.

CRACK! The ball took off, headed for shallow left center field. "I got it! I got it! I got it!" Derek yelled, hoping that Gary could hear him. If not, they were going to have one gigantic collision.

Derek reached for the sinking line drive and grabbed it on the run. But Gary couldn't completely avoid running into Derek, even though he did try to dodge him. His arm hit Derek's glove, knocking the ball out!

Derek knew that all wasn't lost yet. He saw that the ball was still airborne, and did a 180-degree turn, reaching back for it as his momentum pulled him away from it.

The ball landed in his mitt. His mitt hit the ground hard as he came crashing down. But the ball stayed in the glove!

"Yer out!" the umpire yelled.

Ball game over!

Derek windmilled his arms, threw his glove high into the air with the ball still in it, and sank to his knees. He'd just pulled off the play of the season—the play of his *life*, really—to save his team and lead them into the final!

Derek's brain was reeling. A minute ago he'd been feeling sorry for himself. Now he was being mobbed by his teammates. He'd gone from zero to hero, and all in the same inning! He'd saved the team's season, playing a position he hadn't wanted to play—a position *his dad* had put him in!

Derek looked around for his dad, and saw him with his arm around Coach Bradway's shoulders. Both of them were smiling as they watched their team celebrate its victory. Meanwhile, the dejected Twins, out of the playoffs now, were being consoled by their coaches. There were lots of tears, and kids saying, "It's so *unfair*!"

And Dave—where was he? Derek spotted him on the other side of the pile of Indians. It was hard to make his way over there, but Derek wanted to talk to Dave before he ran off and avoided Derek again.

"I need to talk to you," Derek said.

"Right now? I'm—"

"Right now," Derek insisted. "It's like, this is driving me nuts. I mean, don't *you* want to talk about it?"

"About what?"

"See, that's what I mean! You act like everything's normal, but it's not!"

"Okay, okay," Dave said, clearly annoyed. "Come on over here." He led Derek over to the bench and sat down. "I'm listening."

Derek remembered his mother telling him to share his feelings with Dave, then just listen. "I feel like . . . like we're not really friends anymore." If he'd expected Dave to protest, he was disappointed. Dave remained silent, staring at the ground, leaning forward with his elbows on his knees.

"I feel like you don't *want* to be my friend anymore. You keep canceling our plans, and you don't get back to me about the summer. I mean, you don't even come to the Hill these days! If we weren't in class together, or on the team, we'd *never* see each other. And those two things are almost over."

Another silence. "Don't you have anything to say?" Derek finally asked. "Or are you just going to sit there?"

Dave just sat there. Derek couldn't tell if Dave's eyes were welling up with tears or if he was about to explode.

In spite of his mother's advice to share his feelings and then just listen, Derek found himself unable to remain silent. "What is it? Is it your parents who don't like me? Or is it you?"

Dave's fists were clenched tightly. So was his jaw. "And by the way," Derek continued, "if your mom and dad want to spend so much time with you, how come they don't even come to the ball games?"

Suddenly Dave's lips trembled, his eyes overflowed, and he turned to Derek with anger in his face. "Stop asking me all these questions, okay? Don't you think I *want* to come over? Just leave me alone!"

Turning away, he hoisted the bag of bats over his shoulder and marched off in the direction of the big Mercedes, leaving Derek sitting there staring after him.

Chapter Eleven

WHAT'S THE DIFFERENCE?

Vijay was exultant. "We won! Derek, you are the best player in all of Kalamazoo! How did you catch those fly balls? How did you throw that kid out at the plate? You are amazing!"

Derek, while he was happy about the result of the game, was in no mood to be treated like a hero. "Cut it out, okay, Vij?" he said as they got into the back of the station wagon for the ride home.

"What is the matter with you? Don't you realize we are in the final now? We are going to win that big trophy! With you on our team, how can we lose? MVP! MVP!"

Derek was used to this kind of thing from Vijay, who always thought Derek was the best at everything. It was great to have someone think of you that way, he had to admit. But it could be embarrassing—and irritating too sometimes. Like now.

"Stop."

Vijay, suddenly realizing that Derek really, truly wanted him to, quieted down.

"Don't get down on yourself, Derek," said Mr. Jeter from the driver's seat as he eased the wagon into traffic. "Every pitcher has a bad day now and then. And you played great in center."

"I'm not a pitcher," Derek muttered. "I'm not a center fielder. I'm a shortstop."

His dad eyed him sternly in the rearview mirror. "On *this* team you're a *baseball player*," he said, "and your job is to help your team however your coaches tell you to."

Derek felt stung, embarrassed that Vijay was there to witness his dad correcting him. Vijay pretended not to hear, staring out the window at the street.

"Let me remind you again, Derek. You can't control everything, but you can control how you think about it and how you act when things don't go your way. You've got to hang in there and keep after it, not get down and give up. Look how the game turned out today—and you were a big part of it!"

"I guess it's okay . . . because we won."

That seemed to perk Vijay up. "Not only that—we are going to go undefeated all the rest of the way!"

They had arrived outside Vijay's door. "See you soon, Vij," Derek said as they dropped him off.

"You are the best player *ever*!" Vijay said, waving as he walked up the front steps. "Someday you will be famous, Derek. You will see!"

Derek waved back, shaking his head but smiling. Good old Vijay, someone who really believed in him, big-time.

Derek had dreamed since he was a little kid of someday being shortstop for the New York Yankees. It was a big dream—some would have said an impossible dream. In fact, some people *had* said that. But his parents believed in him. And so did Vijay. That helped Derek keep the faith, even when he made an error, or when the dream seemed to be far away and fading fast.

Dave believed in him too. That was how he and Derek had bonded as friends, by believing in each other's dreams. Dave wanted to be a professional golfer some-day, and Derek, who had actually played with him once, believed he could do it.

Derek sighed as his dad parked, and they got out. The big ball of hurt that had grabbed his stomach before the game came roaring back. He used to believe they were best friends, but obviously not. Derek couldn't help but feel that somehow there was something about him that Dave didn't like anymore.

But *what*?

• • •

"All right, class. And now the moment you've been waiting for." Ms. Fein picked up a pile of papers—their math and English finals—and started walking up and down the aisles, handing them back to each student.

Derek felt his breath catch in his throat as he took the papers from his teacher. He squeezed his eyes shut for a moment—then looked.

What? An 87?

To some students an 87 on their English final would have been a great victory. But not for Derek, who was used to scoring at least in the low nineties on English exams. He shuffled the papers and stared at his math final result—91.

At least it's in the nineties, he thought. But really it was an even worse score, considering that math had always been Derek's best subject.

He gazed over at Gary, who didn't seem too happy either. Was it possible that Gary, too, had underperformed? Derek couldn't wait for the bell to ring—in exactly one minute and forty seconds—so he could find out if he'd actually outscored his rival.

In the meantime Derek peeked over at Dave's results—82 in English and 87 in math. And at Vijay's—82 in English and 91 in math.

Vijay was really smart, as Derek well knew. But his English grammar was sometimes off, because he'd learned to speak it from his parents, who were from India and spoke English a bit differently than people born in the US.

He probably would have gotten a 90 otherwise, Derek thought. *It's kind of unfair . . .* Then Derek remembered what his dad had said about unfairness. He guessed Vijay could handle it. At the moment he seemed to be okay with his marks. He was more excited about school letting out than he was upset with his score.

The bell finally rang. Derek followed Gary out into the hallway and walked along beside him as Gary trudged painfully toward their lockers. "What'd you get?" he asked.

Gary paused, reached into his book bag, and took out his test papers to show Derek. "Read 'em and weep, Jeter. A 90 in English and a 94 in Math."

Derek slumped in disappointment.

"Beat you again, huh?" Gary said with a grin that was more like a wince. "Surprise, surprise. I don't know why you even bother, Jeter. I wouldn't waste any tears on it if I were you. You're never going to beat me."

"I did that one time," Derek pointed out.

Gary gave him a smile. "Always looking on the bright side, huh? Oh well. I guess it's 'wait till next year.'"

"Hey, this year's not over yet. We've still got two more finals."

"Yeah, good luck with that," said Gary, continuing on to his locker. "You might as well face facts. You'll never be as smart as me, no matter how hard you study."

"Maybe not, but I can still beat you on a test! This isn't

over, Parnell." Derek's competitiveness was fully awakened now.

It *wasn't* over. He really did believe in his heart that if you want something enough, and you work hard enough at it, you'll get where you want to get. That thought was what kept him going—that if he stuck to it and never gave up, someday he might be out there on the field at Yankee Stadium, leading his team to a World Series Championship.

For now, of course, the Kalamazoo Trophy would have to do. There *was* always next year—that much was true. But *this* year, for the first time in his life, Derek's team had a real shot at the big prize.

As the students gathered their stuff from their lockers, Derek noticed that Gary still looked miserable. "Hey, what's up with you these days, anyway?" he asked. "You seem like you've been really down."

"Down? My life is total misery these days, thanks for asking." He winced as he hoisted his book bag over his shoulder. "I can't wait for math camp to start and rescue me from all this agony. If I hear 'kee-yah' one more time, I'm gonna totally lose my mind."

Wow, thought Derek as he watched Gary limp away. *It's even worse than I thought.*

At dinner that night Derek was doing his best to shake off all thoughts of Dave. He told himself he would still have a ton of fun in New Jersey with just his grandparents and Sharlee.

If only he hadn't gotten his hopes up in the first place. Maybe, he thought, he should ask his parents for something else for his birthday, since he wasn't going to get his first choice.

"How's karate class going, Sharlee?" Mr. Jeter asked.

"Good!" Sharlee said with a wide smile. "I'm the best in the whole class!"

Well, no one in the family was going to argue with her, that was for sure. "I'm glad you like it, Sharlee," said Mrs. Jeter.

"You want to hear something really funny?" Sharlee said. "There's this big kid who's in our class, because he was so bad at karate that they put him in the little kids' class! And you know what, Derek? I think he's on your baseball team!"

Derek's eyes widened. "Gary?"

"Yeah! That's the one. And I'm *way better* at karate than he is!"

"Sharlee, it's not nice to brag," said Mr. Jeter.

"I hope you didn't say anything like that to Gary!" Mrs. Jeter added.

"Sure I did!" Sharlee said, beaming. Then, sensing her parents' disapproval, her smile faded. "I didn't know I wasn't supposed to."

"That's okay," Mrs. Jeter told her. "Just don't do it again, okay? Bragging makes other people feel bad, and it makes you look bad too."

"Oh. Okay. I won't brag anymore, *ever again*," Sharlee said, and just like that, her smile returned.

"What did Gary say when you said that to him?" Derek asked, curious.

"He said, 'Congratulations!'"

"Mmm. Wow." Derek shook his head. No wonder Gary had been so depressed lately!

"So," said their mom, changing the subject. "What's up for you two between now and the end of school?"

"Finals," said Derek with a sigh. "What else?"

"I don't have any finals!" chirped Sharlee.

"So, are you going to be doing something fun in class instead?" asked their mom.

"I think so," said Sharlee, obviously not too sure. "We're doing something this whole week about diversity. We're going to have a big show-and-tell about it on the last day of school." She turned to her mother and said, "Mom, what's diversity?"

"Differences," said Mrs. Jeter.

"What kind of differences?"

"Differences between people. In your classroom you have people who have white skin, brown skin, black skin. . . . You also have girls, like you, and boys, like your brother. And then, if you listen, you might be able to hear someone talk a little differently than you. And all those things, Sharlee, are what diversity is."

"So diversity is just differences in people?"

"Right," said Mrs. Jeter. "Diversity goes even further. There are people who are born in America, and people who are born in other countries, like Derek's friend Vijay. Vijay was born in India, but now his family lives here in America."

"Sharlee," Mr. Jeter added, "we've talked about *our* family before, and how it's different from some of your friends' families. Your mother is white, and I am black. We have a *diverse* household."

"Yeah, Sharlee," Derek said jokingly. "I was born on Earth, and you were born on Mars. We are a very diverse family!"

They all laughed at that one—even Sharlee, who began making martian faces.

"Okay, okay," Mrs. Jeter said, smiling. "Cut it out, the both of you. Quit making me laugh so hard."

"You know what, Sharlee?" said Mr. Jeter. "It so happens I teach a class on Wednesdays at five o'clock that's very diverse. It might give you some information for your show-and-tell—at least the *tell* part. I could pick you up from school and bring you over to my classroom if you want."

"Wow! I can really come?" Sharlee said, clapping. "I get to go to college before you, Derek! Ha-ha!"

Derek laughed and tousled her hair. Sharlee always had the knack of making him forget his troubles.

But that night, lying in bed, Derek got to thinking about

diversity again. He wondered if the reason why Dave was avoiding him was because their families were so different.

The very idea of it made him feel worse than ever. *If that's why,* Derek thought bitterly, *I don't want to be friends with him, either.*

Chapter Twelve

A WORLD OF DIFFERENCE

Derek handed in his science final at five minutes to three. Since it was at the end of the school day and the buses were already outside, students were allowed to leave the classroom when they were done. Derek headed for his locker. Three finals down, one more to go.

Usually he enjoyed school, but right now he couldn't even think about schoolwork. He had no idea how he'd made it this far, much less how he was going to get through the next final.

Luckily, school was almost over for the year. Unluckily, so was baseball season. This coming Saturday would be his birthday, and then . . . what?

Instead of really looking forward to summer in New

Jersey the way he normally did, Derek couldn't help feeling that he wasn't going to have as good a time as usual.

His grandma and all his cousins had always been his playmates while he was in New Jersey. But he was about to turn eleven years old. Big kids needed their best friends around, not just their family. And as great as they were, his grandparents couldn't be expected to keep up with him all day long anymore.

What bothered Derek most was not knowing why Dave had pulled away from their friendship. Four days had passed since the game on Saturday, and he and Derek had barely said two words to each other.

There were still a few kids left in the classroom taking the test, but the buses were already lined up in front. Derek got his book bag from his locker and left the building.

Just before he got to the curb where the buses were waiting, he heard a familiar voice calling him. "Derek."

He turned around to see Chase standing behind him. "Oh . . . hi!"

Usually Chase waited next to the big Mercedes for Dave to come out. But Dave had finished the test ten minutes before Derek had. Why was Chase still here?

Chase cleared his throat. "Derek, Dave has something he'd like to say to you." He turned and gestured to the car, which was parked right behind the buses. Derek walked over to the car, while Chase lagged behind, obviously wanting to give the boys some privacy.

Derek peeked in the rear window of the car, shielding his eyes from the glare of the sun. Just as he did, the window glided down, revealing Dave in the backseat. "Come on in," he said.

Derek got in next to Dave and shut the door behind him. "What's this all about?" he asked.

"First of all, I want to say I'm really sorry about everything . . . about the way I've treated you," Dave said.

Derek shrugged, pretending not to care. "Doesn't matter. I mean, it's not like we're friends anymore."

"Come on, Derek! Of course we're still friends!"

"That's what you think? You sure haven't been acting like it."

"I—I wish I could explain, but believe me—I *do* still want to hang out with you."

"Oh, really? You could have fooled me."

"It just . . . It has to be at my house, okay? We can hang there anytime. You could even come for an overnight! Just . . ."

". . . not at *my* house," Derek finished for him.

Dave bit his lip, then said, "Right."

"I don't know, man. To me, friends aren't friends if they never hang out—and that means at *both* our houses. I've been to your place plenty of times. How come you have a problem with mine?

"I don't!" Dave insisted. "I'm trying to tell you that!"

"But you won't say *why* you can't come to my house."

Dave sighed and looked down at his hands, folded between his knees.

"Well," said Derek, "I'll be around till mid-July, so if you still want to be friends, you can come over to my house, anytime. But after all that's gone down, it has to be at *my* house—at least the next couple of times."

He opened the car door and got out, closed it behind him, and walked back toward the bus. Chase watched him pass, a questioning look on his face. But Derek didn't look back at him. He was too upset to talk to anyone.

Sharlee was more excited than usual at dinner that night. "They all called Daddy 'Professor Jeter'! It was so cool!" she bubbled. "Daddy, is 'professor' the same as 'coach'?"

Mr. Jeter cocked his head in amusement. "Well, not really—but in a way, I guess. Why?"

"Because those grown-ups looked at you just like the kids on Derek's team do."

"They're college students," he corrected her. "Some are grown-ups, some not quite yet."

"Looked at him *how*, exactly?" asked Mrs. Jeter.

"Like he knows everything!" Sharlee crowed. "And he *does* know everything! Right, Daddy?"

"Not even close, Sharlee," said Mr. Jeter. "If you don't believe me, ask your mom." He gave his wife a wink.

"He's right," said Mrs. Jeter. "Your father knows a lot

of things, but there are plenty of things your mom knows that he doesn't."

Everyone laughed—even Derek. Thank goodness for his family, he thought for the millionth time. He knew he could always count on them, in every way.

"So, tell Mom and Derek what happened in class, Sharlee," Mr. Jeter said.

"Well, I know what 'diversity' means now," Sharlee began, taking the floor and commanding everyone's attention. "Daddy's class is full of diversity! There was this lady there with gray hair, and she even has grandchildren—and she's in college! And there's a boy from Afghanistan and a girl from Indonesia. And they have accents. And there was a guy in a wheelchair, too. And there were black students and white ones and Asian ones and Hispanic ones. . . ."

"That certainly is diverse!" said Mrs. Jeter.

"And, oh! There was this blind girl?" Sharlee went on. "She's one of Daddy's students too, and she told us all about what it's like—how you have to learn to get around without seeing anything. We even had to close our eyes for a few minutes and walk around the classroom and stuff, so we could get an idea of what it's like for her."

"Wonderful!" Mrs. Jeter exclaimed. "Were you surprised, Sharlee?"

"It wasn't easy, but I did it. I only bumped into one or two things!" Sharlee said, forgetting her promise never to brag again. Then her smile faded suddenly as she remembered something else.

"But then she said it didn't matter how much she could do. People still looked at her and saw a *blind* person—not a *person*. And she said people made fun of her when she was little, and sometimes didn't want to be friends with her. That made me sad. And then she told Daddy how beautiful I was. I asked Daddy how she could know that without seeing me, and he said I should ask her myself. So I did!"

"And what did she tell you, Sharlee?" Mr. Jeter asked.

"She said she could tell from my voice. It was *amazing*! I never knew you could tell if someone was pretty by listening to their voice!"

"That *is* amazing, Sharlee!" said Mrs. Jeter. "And just think, if you hadn't asked her, you would never have known!"

"Yeah," Sharlee agreed. "I always thought blind people couldn't do anything, but it turns out they can do amazing things, and we don't even notice."

"Well, Sharlee," said Mr. Jeter, "I hope you learned that just because some people are different from us doesn't mean they don't have a lot to give, or aren't worthy of friendship and respect."

"Uh-huh," Sharlee said, nodding sagely.

"So what are you going to tell your class for show-and-tell?" Derek asked her.

"I'm going to tell them that in Daddy's classroom

everyone is different from everyone else, but everyone's also the same. They're all amazing people, and if you get to know them, they're not as different as they seem." She looked around the room. "Is that okay?"

"Yes, honey," said her dad, smiling. "That's just fine."

"And it's not just in Daddy's classroom" said Mrs. Jeter. "It's everyone, everywhere."

His dad knocked on the bathroom door as Derek was brushing his teeth. "There was something else I wanted to say down there," he said.

"What?" Derek asked.

"Just that we were talking about diversity so that Sharlee could understand it. But at your age, as I'm sure you know, diversity is a much larger discussion, and much more complicated. There's differences in how much money people have, there are people living with disabilities, there are different traditions and cultures that might seem strange till you get to know them better . . ." He searched Derek's face to see if he got the point.

Derek wanted to ask him if he thought diversity was what Dave's parents were so worked up about. But his mouth was full of toothpaste, so he just nodded that he understood. His dad nodded back, said good night, and closed the door behind him.

Derek finished washing up, but he kept thinking about what his dad had said—and about Dave's family. The

Hennums had lots of money, and probably all their friends did too. The Jeters weren't rich. Not only that, but they were an interracial family.

Could that be it? Derek thought. He hated to think so—even though he knew that there were people in the world who still judged people as "types," not as people. He sure hoped that wasn't true of the Hennums.

Chapter Thirteen

WHAT IS A FRIEND?

After school on Thursday—which was more or less an all-day study session, with breaks for gym, music, and art—Derek and Vijay met on the Hill.

They started tossing a baseball back and forth, because they were the only ones there. Summer vacation was less than a week away, and Little League season was over for most kids—the ones whose teams weren't in the final.

Gary could have been out there with them, although he probably would have found some excuse not to be. But as Derek knew, Gary was in karate class today, with Sharlee and the other little kids.

Life really stank for Gary right now, Derek thought, shaking his head. Of course, that didn't mean he wouldn't come to school ready to beat Derek on their social studies final.

And Dave wasn't there with them either—surprise, surprise. Derek lobbed the ball back toward Vijay, but missed by a mile, his mind distracted by dark thoughts.

"What's up with you today?" Vijay asked as he ran to retrieve the ball from under one of the two trees that made the Hill such a bizarre place to play baseball. The trees were in awkward places—one in fair territory in left field, the other just off the foul line in right.

"I don't know," Derek said, although of course he knew perfectly well what was bothering him.

"Well, I *do* know your mind is one million miles away." Vijay came over and sat down on the rock that served as home plate. "And I don't think friends should keep secrets from each other."

Derek winced. "Okay, you caught me, Vij. You're right, as usual. I was thinking about Dave again."

"Are you still best friends with him?" Vijay asked.

Derek shrugged. "I guess not. Not by the way he's been acting, anyway."

Vijay nodded slowly. "He doesn't ask to hang out with me anymore either."

Just weeks ago Derek's mom had been referring to the three of them as the Three Musketeers, because they'd been spending so much time together.

"It's really weird," Vijay commented. "And for no reason at all!"

"I don't know. I think there *is* a reason. I feel like his parents might not like us very much."

Vijay nodded thoughtfully. "When my family first came here to Kalamazoo from India, not everybody welcomed us. I think they made up their minds about us without even meeting us and getting to know us." He stared out into the distance, remembering.

"Maybe it was our skin color, or the way we dressed, or our accents, or the smells of my mom's cooking. Her food did make the hallway smell nice, but I guess some people weren't used to it."

Derek nodded. He would never forget the first time he'd met Vijay. He remembered seeing Vijay across the playground, all by himself while everyone else was busy having fun, playing with one another and ignoring the newcomer. Derek had gone over and introduced himself, and Vijay had broken out into the biggest, happiest smile Derek had ever seen.

"If it hadn't been for you and your parents, who knows how it all would have turned out," Vijay went on. "But once you made friends with us, everybody else must have decided it was okay—because now we have more friends here than anybody else!"

He shot Derek that same big smile, and Derek couldn't help returning it. "You know something, Vij? Making friends with you was the best move I ever made."

He clapped Vijay on the shoulder, then asked, "So, do

you think I'm right about Dave's parents? That they don't want him to be friends with us because our families are so different?"

"It may be," Vijay said with a sad shrug of his shoulders. "Or maybe you've got it all wrong."

But Derek was pretty well convinced that he *wasn't* wrong. "Why are people *like* that?" he asked. "Why can't people be friends—best friends—even if they *are* different? I mean, you and I are different, and *we're* best friends, right?"

"Right!" Vijay replied. "I wish I could tell you for sure why people are like that, but who knows?"

Seeing the hurt look on Derek's face, Vijay said, "Listen, I know it's not fair. Nobody knows that better than I do. But you can't do anything about what's in other people's hearts. All we can do is be ourselves and trust that Dave still wants to be friends."

"It doesn't matter what *he* wants. It's what his *parents* want that counts."

"We will see about that," said Vijay. "But I tell you one thing for sure—if he really wants to be friends with you, he will find a way."

Derek glanced over at Gary, who had his head buried in his test paper. Then Gary looked up and glanced at Derek. Derek swiftly looked back down at his own paper. He was determined to finish before his rival. Not only was he going to beat Gary on the test, but he was going to finish first too!

Derek didn't want to make a mistake on any of the last few questions, but he didn't want to take too much time either. Bragging rights mattered in this little war of theirs, and Gary almost always won. But Derek never gave up and was always determined to come back next time and compete even harder.

Derek finished the last answer and slapped his pencil down onto his desk. At the same moment he saw that Gary was rising to his feet. They'd finished at exactly the same time!

Both boys went up to the teacher and handed in their papers, then headed for the door. Derek just beat him there. "Ha! First one out!" he said playfully. But Gary didn't fire back.

"Good for you, Jeter. You win. Pretty immature, though, especially considering I'm going to beat you on the final anyway."

"Oh yeah? We'll see about that." Derek was reasonably sure he'd aced this one.

As they approached their lockers, Derek saw two older boys coming down the hallway toward them. He thought they might be sixth graders, but they could even have been in seventh.

"Hey, Karate Kid!" one of them called out, recognizing Gary.

Gary stopped cold, frozen to the spot.

"Yo, Flab-a-thon!" the other said, holding up a hand as if to high-five Gary, but at the last minute yanking it away and pretending to do a series of karate chops on Gary's body. "Kee-yah! Yah! Yah!"

Gary tried to protect himself—even though the kid wasn't really touching him. Still, that seemed to rev the two boys up even more. "Broken any toothpicks lately, Bruce Lee?" the first kid joked. He and his buddy high-fived each other, yukking it up.

Derek watched as Gary stood there and took it, not saying a word to his two tormentors. But Derek was sick and tired of people hurting other people's feelings, and he wasn't going to just let these boys get away with it.

Derek felt the urge to slug them but quickly restrained himself. He remembered what had happened the time he'd tried to deal with a bully who was picking on Sharlee. Derek had grabbed him by the shirt, pushed him up against a wall, and warned him to cut it out.

But it was Derek who had wound up getting in trouble, with the school *and* with his parents. Worst of all, he'd been ashamed, for acting like a bully himself.

"Hey, Gary," he said. "Who are these clowns, anyway? You know them?"

"They're in karate class," Gary said, eyeing the two warily.

"The *big kid* karate class," the first one said. "Where

everybody is at least ten years old and has a yellow belt—including us. Hey, Klutzo, do they even give out belts in the baby class?"

"It's not the *baby* class!" Gary finally shot back. "It's the *beginner* class!"

"Yeah, and you're the only beginner in it who's older than six!" the second boy said, setting off another round of high fives and laughs.

Derek stepped between them and Gary. "You know what? You guys ought to be ashamed of yourselves, picking on someone just because he's at a different level in karate."

"*Different?* I'll say he's different," said the first kid. "Hey, Blobbo, can you break this?" More laughter as he waved a pencil at Gary.

"His name's not 'Blobbo.' It's not 'Klutzo.' It's *Gary*. He happens to be a friend of mine. And let me tell you, you've got him all wrong."

"Oh yeah?" said the second kid. "Like how?"

"He might be new at karate, but it's only a matter of time with Gary, because he's such a great athlete." Derek glanced at Gary, whose jaw was hanging open in surprise.

"Yeah, right," said the first boy.

"Did you know he's a heck of a baseball player?" Derek went on. "It's only his first season, but he's already practically our MVP! He worked out so hard that he gained ten pounds of pure muscle, and now he can outhustle anyone else on the team! Oh, and by the way, he got us the big hit the other day that put us into the finals!"

None of it was *exactly* true—but hey, it might turn out to be true, right? By the end of the season, Gary might really be their MVP! Stranger things had happened, after all—although most of them were featured in *Ripley's Believe It or Not!*

At any rate Derek was on a roll and was in no mood to stop now. "You know what else? He's actually making a lot of progress in karate."

"WHAT?" the boys said in unison.

"Yup. Go on, Gary. Show 'em how you can flip me."

Gary was now totally slack-jawed. Derek gave him a secret wink, making sure the two boys couldn't see it. "Go on. *Show* 'em."

Gary moved slowly forward and grabbed Derek's extended wrist in both his hands. "Just what do you think you're doing?" he whispered. "Are you crazy?"

"Shh, trust me." Derek whispered back. Then he said out loud, "Okay, go!"

Gary raised his hands up and brought them down again. Derek cried out in surprise as he did a forward flip—all on his own power, of course—and rolled out flat on the ground, groaning in faked pain. He had been practicing this bit with Sharlee, and he did a fantastic acting job.

"Whoa!" the two boys said, their eyes wide.

"I had no idea, man!" said the first one, going over to Gary and clapping him on the arm. "That was awesome! My bad."

"So what are you doing in the little kids' class?" asked the second one.

"Uhh . . ." Gary looked stumped, so Derek came to the rescue with another well-timed fib.

"He's coaching my little sister! And you should see her. She could flip either one of you, easy!"

"Huh. Well. I guess . . . we got you wrong, Parnell," said the first boy.

"Yeah," said the second. "You're okay, man. We should hang out sometime, and you can teach me that flip. It's pretty cool."

After the two of them had gone, Derek got up and dusted himself off. "You okay?" Gary asked him. "You looked like you hurt yourself there."

"That's acting, Gar," said Derek, taking a bow.

"Nice job. You ought to get an Academy Award."

"Practice makes perfect," said Derek with a grin.

"Wait a minute, though," said Gary, holding up an index finger. "You called me your *friend* just then."

"Yeah. I guess I did, huh?"

"I assume that was all part of the act, right?"

"Well . . . yes and no. . . . I mean we *are*—kind of . . . in a way . . ."

"I don't get it, Jeter," said Gary, shaking his head. "After all the crud I always put you through, why'd you stick up for me?"

Derek smiled. "You know what, Gar? I've been in your shoes. People judging us without knowing us? Besides," he added, "it just didn't seem right. I don't like it when people act like jerks."

"Well, I hope you don't mean me!" Gary said, half-joking.

"You just said you put me through crud," Derek pointed out with a grin. "But hey, no, I didn't mean you."

"Listen," Gary said. "Seriously, that was pretty awesome of you. So at least let me pay you a compliment. You, Jeter, are definitely smarter than the average bear."

"Gee, thanks, buddy!" Derek said. "You finally admitted it! So . . . friends?" He stuck his hand out for Gary to shake.

Gary just looked at it. "Don't get any ideas," he said. "Just because we're 'friends' now, it doesn't mean I'm gonna act any different in the future. You're still the competition, as far as I'm concerned—except on the Indians."

But then he *did* shake Derek's hand.

"See you tomorrow," Derek told him. "This one's for the league championship, so don't be late. I told those two jokers you could outhustle anybody on the team—so don't make a liar out of me!"

"You got it," Gary agreed. "I'll be there, ready to rumble."

"Hey, you know what, Gary? If you actually put a little

effort into it, you really could flip me—or even those two guys."

"Hmm," Gary said thoughtfully. "Not a bad idea. I've actually got karate class later today. . . . Thanks for the thought, Jeter."

Chapter Fourteen

THIS MAGIC MOMENT

"Fair ball!"

"Noooo!" It wasn't just Derek moaning. It was every single Indian, and all their fans in the bleachers. "That ball was foul by at least six inches!"

Derek had run into short left field to get it—and had almost collided with Gary, who was playing the position that Gary called "left out."

Afraid of a collision, Derek had pulled up at the last moment, and the ball had fallen between them. It had ricocheted off Gary's shin before bouncing farther into foul territory. Gary now howled in pain, grabbing his leg.

"Fair ball!" the umpire yelled again. Derek ran to retrieve the ball. He and Gary had both clearly seen it land foul. Unluckily for the Indians, the ump couldn't see through them. He'd had to call the play blind, and he'd missed it!

With the bases loaded and two out, all three Giants runners had been running on the play. By the time Derek managed to get to the ball and throw it back in, it was too late. The third runner scored all the way from first base, just beating the tag, and giving the Giants an early 3–0 lead with a man on second.

Everyone on the Indians slumped, like balloons with all the air let out of them. Their pitcher was affected by it too. Dave walked the next batter on four straight pitches. Coach Jeter quickly called time-out and ran out to the mound to calm his pitcher down before this game got completely away from them.

Derek came over from short to listen in. "It's so *unfair*!" Dave was saying. "That ball was foul by a mile!"

Derek knew what his dad was going to say next, so he was not surprised at the coach's words. Why should he have been? Hadn't both coaches been preaching the same thing all season?

"You can't control the breaks," Derek's dad told Dave. "You can only control yourself. That walk you just issued— that happened because *you* let a bad call throw you off your game. Now it's too late to change that, but let's get this next guy out, okay? Just throw strikes, make him hit it, and trust your fielders to do the rest." After clapping

Dave on the shoulder, he returned to the bench.

Derek went back to short. He'd noticed even before the game that Dave looked unusually downcast. This unlucky break, so early in the biggest game of his life, had clearly shaken him up even more.

But the coach's visit seemed to have steadied him. Dave threw two straight strikes, then got the hitter to ground out to second to end the top of the first.

"Okay, Indians!" Coach Jeter clapped each member of his team on the back as they returned to the bench. "Let's not get down now! We've got a game to win—an all-or-nothing game, with the league championship at stake. We've got to be playing our best. That means we can't let bad breaks ruin our concentration, or our will! Come on now. Let's get ourselves back into this game!"

Derek could feel the seriousness of the moment. With all his troubles during the last few weeks, he too had struggled to give his best effort, whether in school or on the field.

But he knew that for the next two hours, if he wanted to be a champion for the first time in his life, he had to put everything else out of his head. Everything.

Looking around at his teammates, he could only hope they would all take his dad's words to heart.

Mason started the team on a high note, with another walk. He'd been getting them all season, and this one took nine pitches. "Way to work it!" Coach Bradway shouted, and the Indians all cheered as Mason jogged down the base line.

Everyone knew what would come next. Dean would take a strike and give Mason a chance to steal second. Sure enough, on the second pitch, with a 1–0 count, the catcher dropped the ball in the dirt, and Mason slid into second ahead of the throw.

The Indians whooped it up, even though they were still down by three runs. To Derek that was a good sign. It meant they hadn't given up. And why should they? They hadn't come this far by being a bad team, after all.

Dean hit a sharp grounder. Even though the second baseman made a great play on it and threw him out at first, Mason managed to get to third.

Derek pulled the brim of his batting helmet down low over his eyes. He didn't want the glare from the sunny sky getting in the way of his seeing the ball. With a man on third, he told himself not to be greedy and try to hit a home run. All the team needed was a fly ball to the outfield, and they'd be on the comeback trail.

Derek took two strikes, because they were down at the knees and hard to hit into the air. After ball one the next pitch was high and only a little outside. Derek reached out and slapped it over the first baseman's head for a base hit—and the Indians' first run!

Rounding first, Derek clapped his hands in satisfaction. "Let's go, Dave!" he shouted. "Keep the line moving!"

But Dave swung at a pitch up in his eyes and popped up to the pitcher for the second out.

Next to hit was Tito. He hit a line drive right at the left fielder, who barely had to move to make the catch.

So in the end the Indians were forced to settle for one run. But at least they hadn't given up after that first three-run outburst against them. There were still five innings left, Derek told himself, plenty of time for a comeback.

But first they had to hold back the Giants, who had scored more runs this season than any other team. Luckily, Dave settled into a nice rhythm on the mound and retired the next six Giants in a row.

For their part, the Indians did their best to mount a rally in their half of the second, loading the bases on a hit and two walks but failing to score when Dean popped out to third to end the inning.

In the bottom of the third, with the Indians still down 3–1, it was Derek's turn to lead off. He told himself he had to get on base, somehow, some way. He also knew that if the Indians didn't start hitting soon, this might even be his last at bat of the season!

Derek was determined not to let that happen. He hadn't spent all those hours in the batting cages for nothing. His dad had shown him how to hit an inside pitch the other way, toward the right side of the field. You had to keep your hands in, close to your chest, and pull them forward first, so that when the bat hit the ball, the bat was pointed toward right field.

The first pitch was in the dirt. Derek almost swung, but he held up at the last moment. He reminded himself not to swing at anything that wasn't a strike. After all, a walk was as good as a hit when you were leading off an inning.

On the next pitch Derek saw the ball coming in at him, high enough so he could put his inside-out swing on it. He made solid contact, and the ball shot right between the second and first basemen for a single!

Derek had never been so psyched just to reach first base. And his success seemed to inspire the rest of the team too. Dave followed with a rocket that split the out-fielders, scoring Derek all the way from first to make it 3–2!

With a runner on second, Tito hit a sharp grounder that got through the infield, and Dave beat the throw home while Tito got to second on the throw. Tie game, and still no one out!

Two hard ground balls were turned into two outs by sparkling plays in the infield. But Tito made it to third on the first one, and scored on the second, to give the Indians their first lead of the game, 4–3!

"YEAH!" Derek screamed. He was starting to go hoarse from cheering. By the end of the game, he'd probably have no voice left, but he didn't care, as long as they won!

Gary swung for the fences on a slow pitch, and popped

out to first base to end the inning. But now the Indians had the lead.

All they had to do was keep it, and they would be league champions. But it soon became clear it wasn't going to be that easy—not by a long shot.

By the top of the fifth, Dave was tiring, and nearing his pitch limit. He walked two batters before getting a ground ball out that advanced the runners to second and third. Now the Giants' cleanup hitter came to the plate, looking to turn the game back around with one big swing.

Maybe it was fatigue, or maybe it was fear, but Dave's pitches were all outside, and he walked his third man of the inning. That brought Coach Jeter out to the mound, and he signaled for Derek to take over, while Jonathan moved from third to short, and Dave went to play third base in his place.

Now it was all up to *him*, Derek realized. With the bases loaded and only one out, there was no room for error. He was going to have to strike these two hitters out—or hope against hope that if they hit the ball, it would turn into a double play.

Derek worked the count to 2–2 with fastballs, then risked a changeup. He left it up in the zone—a bad mistake—but the hitter was fooled by the slowness of the pitch, and struck out swinging!

One down, one more to go, thought Derek. He could feel his heart racing and the sweat trickling down the sides of his face.

He got ahead of the hitter with strike one. But then he made a mistake, throwing an inside pitch that hit the batter. The tying run scored, and the bases were still loaded!

Derek wanted to sink into the ground and disappear, but he heard his father's voice from the bench, yelling, "Hang in there, Derek! Keep it where it is, and we'll get that run back!"

Derek forced himself to calm down. He threw another changeup for a strike, then two fastballs down at the knees, for a three-pitch strikeout to end the Giants' rally and keep the score tied.

His teammates congratulated him, but Derek didn't respond. He could have kicked himself for letting in the tying run!

The Indians went down one, two, three in their half of the fifth. But Derek stood tall on the mound in the top of the sixth, getting the Giants on three straight fly balls.

So, even though he'd blown the lead, the Indians came up in the bottom of the sixth with a chance to walk off as winners. "Come on, guys!" Derek urged his teammates with whatever voice he had left. "This is our shot. Let's do it!"

Amazingly, it fell to him to lead off again and get yet another rally going. This time, he noticed, the Giants were playing him straightaway, not giving him any obvious gaps to shoot for.

Aha, they've caught on, he thought. *Okay, I'll just have to hit it where they can't reach it!*

He worked himself into a 2–1 count. Knowing the pitcher didn't want to fall behind, 3–1, and risk walking the leadoff man, Derek got ready to put his hardest swing on the next pitch.

As he'd expected, it was right down the middle—the fastest pitch the Giants' pitcher could throw. But this was not their starter. Because of pitch limits, the Giants had had to make a substitution, putting a reliever in for this last crucial inning, and this kid did not have the same kind of strike-'em-out stuff.

Derek launched the pitch into the outfield. The center fielder and left fielder both converged on it. But the ball had been hit much harder than they'd realized. It got past both of them and kept on going!

When he saw the ball get through the outfielders, Derek was already on his way to second. Now he kicked it into an even higher gear, rounded third, and slid into home plate with the winning run, while the ball was still on its way back in from the outfield!

The victorious Indians erupted into joyful celebration, throwing their mitts and caps into the air. Forming a big huddle at home plate, they jumped up and down, with Derek right in the middle of it all.

Champions! They were champions—and so was *he*. Derek was numb but was just beginning to grasp the amazing reality.

Finally! One of his life's big dreams had come true, and

it had been his home run that had made the difference. He made his way out of the crowd and looked for his dad, who was in the stands, hugging his mom and Sharlee. Derek ran right over to them.

"Thanks, Dad!" Derek said, hugging his father tightly. "I *knew* we'd win with you as our coach!"

"Hey," said Mr. Jeter, "it was *you* who did it—you and the rest of the guys. But don't forget. We've still got one more big game to go! You *do* want that first annual Kalamazoo Trophy, don't you?"

"YES!" Derek yelled, although barely any sound came out of his hoarse throat.

"Well, then don't let up now!" said his dad, patting him on the back and adding, "Great game today, Derek. This is one you can put in your scrapbook and remember forever."

Derek saw Coach Bradway and went over to thank him, too. Chase high-fived him and said, "Congratulations, Derek. Way to hang in there and turn things around."

Dave came over to high-five Chase too. When he saw Derek, Dave hesitated for a brief second, then reached out and gave him a quick hug. "We did it, man," he said. "We really did it."

"Yup." Derek gave Dave a quick, tight-lipped smile, then turned and walked away.

It was a great, shining moment, no doubt about it. But the cloud that still hovered between them darkened the brightness of a day that should have been filled with sunshine—the day they won the Westwood Little League championship and made their way into the Kalamazoo Trophy game.

Afterward the two coaches treated all the Indians to ice cream at Jahn's. There were speeches, trophies given out, a surprise birthday cake for Derek, and a reminder from Coach Jeter that they still had one very big game to play—and another, bigger trophy to shoot for.

Chapter Fifteen

BREAKING POINT

School let out early on Monday. Derek climbed onto the bus for the ride home, and was surprised when Dave got on too and made his way down the aisle to sit next to Derek.

"Hi," Dave said.

"What's up?" Derek asked him. "You never take the bus home."

"Yeah, my mom needed Chase to pick her up at noon downtown and drive her home, so I said I'd get back on my own."

"Oh. Okay, cool." It still seemed weird to Derek that Dave was here on the bus, and sitting next to him. After all the time Dave had spent avoiding Derek's company lately, it was a shift, for sure.

"Well, this is where I get off," Derek told Dave as the bus approached Mount Royal.

"What are you up to this afternoon?" Dave asked him.

"Not much. I was just going to watch the Tigers-Yankees game at one. Why?"

"Is it . . . okay if I come over for a while?"

"Uh . . . sure, I guess . . ." This was getting stranger and stranger. "Is Chase going to come pick you up later?"

Dave shrugged and got up to follow Derek off the bus. They made their way into the complex and over to the Jeters' townhouse.

There was a note taped to the door. Derek took it down and read it:

Hi, Old Man. Dad had to go clean out his office at school for the term, and I need to pick up a few things on my way home from getting Sharlee. If you get this, it's because I'm running a little late. Make yourself a peanut butter sandwich and I'll be back in a few minutes. Love, Mom.

"Looks like no one's home yet," Derek said as they entered. Dave came in and stood there, waiting for Derek to say something else.

"It's . . . it's great you came," he finally said. "I was starting to think you didn't want to be friends anymore." He laughed, but there was no humor in it.

"No, man!" Dave protested. "I do want to be friends! Of course I do. It's just been . . . crazy."

"You want some water or something? Some juice?"

Derek led Dave into the kitchen, where he poured them each some apple juice and they sat down at the table opposite each other.

"So how long can you stay?" Derek asked. "Is Chase coming to get you after he takes your mom home?"

Dave heaved a huge sigh. "He doesn't know I'm here. And, actually . . . neither do my parents." He took a deep breath. "I just . . . I couldn't take it anymore."

"Huh?"

"You're my best friend. *Ever.* And if they don't want me to come over here, too bad!"

Derek sat in silent shock for a moment. It *was* Dave's parents who were responsible for the gulf that had opened up between them.

"Well, say *something*," Dave begged.

"I . . . I'm glad you came. But you shouldn't have come without permission, without telling anybody. They're going to be worried about you."

"I don't care. It's just not fair!"

"Man, you are seriously disobeying your parents. I'm glad to see you, and I'm really happy you want to hang out, but . . . well, think of what's going to happen when they find out. They'll never let you come over here again!"

Dave was silent, brooding over what Derek had just said. "I guess you're right. But they weren't going to let me come, so . . . Anyway, it's too late now."

"Hey, you hungry?" Derek asked, not knowing what else

to say. "We've got PB and J. I could make you a sandwich."

Derek started making him a sandwich. While he worked, he thought about what Dave had said, that it was so *unfair*. He remembered what his parents said every time that word came up—that Derek could only control his *own* actions. Well, that was what Dave had done, wasn't it? Control his own actions?

Derek was glad about it, because it showed that Dave still wanted to be friends. But he still wondered if it had been the best way to handle things. . . .

He heard the front door open, and his mom come in, followed by Sharlee, shouting, "Kee-yah! Kee-yah!"

Uh-oh, Derek thought. *Here goes nothing.*

"Dave!" Mrs. Jeter gasped as she came into the kitchen and saw him sitting there. "What a nice surprise!"

"Hi, Dave," said Sharlee. "Are you and Derek friends again?"

Dave couldn't help smiling. "Sure, Sharlee. We never stopped being friends."

"Funny, I didn't see Chase when I came in," said Mrs. Jeter. "He usually waits out there with the car. Did he drop you off? Are you staying for dinner?"

"I, uh . . ." Dave swallowed hard. "I . . . I came here on my own, Mrs. Jeter. My parents and Chase don't know where I am. I just . . . wanted to come over and see Derek. I felt like we needed to talk some stuff out."

"I understand, Dave. And it's always good to talk things

over. But you know you shouldn't be running off places without an adult's permission." She reached for the wall phone.

"Mom, wait!" Derek pleaded.

"Don't, Mrs. Jeter!" Dave begged. "I won't stay long, I promise."

"I'm sorry, Dave," she said, kindly but firmly. "That's not how we do things around here. They're your parents, and when they're not here, Chase is in charge of your care. Sneaking around behind their backs is never appropriate, no matter how good a reason you think you have."

She punched in the number and waited. "Hello? . . . Oh, hello, Mrs. Hennum. This is Dorothy Jeter—Derek's mother? . . . Yes, hi. . . . Yes, I have. He's right here in our kitchen."

Derek and Dave both sat at the little table, their heads resting in their hands.

". . . Yes. . . . No, I knew nothing about it. I just came home and found him here with Derek. . . . Right. Very good. We'll be right here waiting. . . . Bye-bye now."

She hung up and folded her arms across her chest. "She'll be here in twenty minutes. She sounded quite upset, I'm afraid. I hope you both understand why."

Chapter Sixteen

MOMENT OF TRUTH

"Hey, Derek, can I show Dave how I can flip you?" They'd been practicing their trick together every day, and it never failed to delight her.

"Not right now, Sharlee," Derek said gloomily, glancing over at Dave. "I'm kind of tired."

"Awww . . ." She pouted for a moment, then remembered something. "Oh! By the way, that kid Gary? He's not in my karate class anymore. He went back in with the big kids."

"He did? How come?"

"He came in and broke two boards with his bare foot!"

"What? No way!"

"Yes way! Two at the same time! Sensei said he's going to get a belt and everything."

Derek couldn't believe it. Obviously, after their experience at school the other day, Gary had decided to show those bullies the real Karate Kid!

"Sharlee, leave the boys alone," Mrs. Jeter said. "Remember, you promised to clean your room today."

"Awww . . ." Back to pouting, Sharlee went upstairs.

Derek and Dave stared out the living room window as the Mercedes pulled into the parking lot. Chase got out and opened the rear door for Mrs. Hennum. She was wearing a business suit and carrying a fancy leather handbag. She said something to Chase, who looked over at Derek and Dave and nodded.

Mrs. Jeter went outside to greet them. She and Mrs. Hennum exchanged a quick handshake, and Mrs. Jeter invited her inside with a wave of her arm.

As they entered the house, Mrs. Hennum spotted Dave. "David, please wait with Chase outside. Mrs. Jeter and I would like to speak in private."

Mrs. Jeter nodded at Derek, indicating that she wanted him to go with Dave. Derek would have wanted to stay around and hear what they said. But he wasn't going to protest. He followed Dave out the door. The two boys went over to Chase, who was polishing the hood of the Mercedes.

"Well, boys, it looks like you've gotten yourselves into some hot water, eh?" Chase gave them a sympathetic look. "Reminds me of a time when I was in the service and we got into hot water with our major by going off base one evening. Have I ever told you that one, Dave?"

Dave shook his head, and Chase began to tell them the story, which went on and on and on. Derek barely paid attention. All he could think about was what was going on inside his house.

Dave seemed distracted too, and after a long while Chase seemed to notice. He stopped before the end of the story and said, "Well, maybe you boys would rather hear about my time in the minor leagues. It was after I got out of the service and before I got my present job. Of course, I never got very far in baseball—couldn't hit the curve, I came to find out. But . . ." His baseball stories would normally have greatly interested Derek, but not today.

What are they talking about in there? he thought. *It's taking forever!* Underneath it all, Derek dreaded what was going to come next. Probably a complete ban on him and Dave being friends, he thought sadly.

And why? What had he done that was so bad? What had *Dave* done, except sneak over just now? And he'd only done it because he was desperate to have friends in Kalamazoo! It was all so *unfair*!

Derek found it hard to pay attention. He just had to know what they were saying in there! There *had* to be a way to get inside and listen in. . . .

"Um, Chase?" he said, suddenly getting a brilliant idea. "I have to go to the bathroom. *Really badly.*"

"Hmmm." Chase glanced quickly at his watch. "Can you wait just a few more minutes? I'm sure they're almost done in there."

"It's an emergency!"

"Well . . ." Chase took a moment to think it over. "I guess if you've got to go, you've got to go. But make sure you head straight for the bathroom and come straight back out. No detours—got it?"

"Yes, sir," Derek said, almost saluting—and quickly made a dash for the front door. He opened it and saw that no one was in the living room. He could hear voices coming from the kitchen, and he supposed that his mom was sitting at the table with Mrs. Hennum.

He went quietly down the hall to the bathroom. He went inside but didn't close the door, because from here he could hear some of what their moms were saying.

He didn't really have to use the bathroom that badly, he decided. It could wait. And anyway, flushing would have alerted them to the fact that he was there. So he just stood there for as long as he thought he could stretch it—which wasn't more than a minute or two, because he knew Chase would be expecting him back soon.

"When I was growing up . . . ," he heard Mrs. Hennum say, but couldn't hear the rest. Here and there words came through—"differences" and "social circles."

Derek heard his mom say something about "breaking barriers" in reply, but he lost the rest of that, too. He had to get closer in order to hear more, but did he dare risk being discovered?

He knew he should just head back outside. If he stayed any longer, there was a good chance he might get caught. But Derek couldn't resist lingering for just one more minute He edged closer to the kitchen door, moving on tiptoe.

"I would hope," his mom was saying, "that we wouldn't allow the way we grew up to affect our kids. They seem to be great friends, with a lot in common."

"Yes, I agree, that is true," said Mrs. Hennum. "And I am sorry that it's all blown up this way."

"Well, I wish you would have just asked me, or come over and gotten to know us if there were any concerns. Honestly, we're no different from any other family. We may look different from some families, but we love and care for our children the same way I'm sure you do. We have rules in our home, just as you do. We're a very close-knit family, and we're very supportive of one another."

"Yes. I can see that," Mrs. Hennum replied. "You know, Mrs. Jeter—"

"Dorothy. Please."

Derek knew he couldn't risk staying any longer. He quickly tiptoed back down the hall and across the living room, opened the front door, and closed it softly behind him. "They're still talking," he told Chase.

Finally Dave's mother emerged from the house. "David,

get into the car, please. It's time to go home," she said, coming down the steps and walking toward them.

Derek and Dave looked at each other. Was this the end of their friendship once and for all? It certainly looked that way.

Then Derek's mom stepped into the doorway. Mrs. Hennum turned to her and said, "Dorothy, we'll see you when we drop David off for the overnight." Turning to Derek, she added, "If that's okay with you, Derek!"

Derek couldn't have been more flabbergasted if a martian had suddenly appeared in front of him. He looked at Dave, wide-eyed and open-mouthed, and saw that Dave, too, was in a state of shock. Neither of them could believe their good luck.

"You have a very fine mother, young man," Mrs. Hennum told Derek. "I'm glad we finally got a chance to get to know each other." She gave Mrs. Jeter a quick smile, and Derek saw that his mom was nodding in agreement. "Chase? I think we're ready to go home!"

Chase opened the rear doors for Mrs. Hennum and Dave, then got into the driver's seat and pulled the Mercedes out of the parking lot.

Derek looked at his mom, still dumbfounded. She gave him a mysterious little smile, cocked her head, and went back inside without a word.

Derek watched the car disappear down the road. It felt really good, knowing that Dave had never wanted to break off their friendship. And he felt even *better* knowing that neither, in the end, had his parents.

For once Derek felt great to have been wrong. *Funny,* he thought, *that's just what Mrs. Hennum said.*

Best of all, he and Dave were finally going to have their overnight!

Chapter Seventeen
ENDINGS AND BEGINNINGS

Today was Tuesday, the last day of school, and Ms. Fein was busy handing back their science and social studies finals. This was the last bit of school business before the class spent the day having their end-of-year party.

Derek was in the mood for partying. He and Dave had already set up their overnight for Wednesday, right after the big championship game that would decide the Kalamazoo Trophy.

Derek sure hoped they would win, because if they didn't, he and Dave would both be bummed out, and that would take a lot of the fun out of their overnight.

But Derek didn't think that would happen. He had always believed his dad would lead their team to the championship, and nothing had happened yet to dent that faith.

As part of his birthday celebrations, his parents had already said they would take Derek and any three friends of his choice to the batting cages this weekend—followed by pizza at A.J.'s. Vijay and Dave were already on board, and Derek was debating whom else to invite.

Ms. Fein stopped at his desk. "Very nice work, Derek. I can see you studied hard." She gave him his papers and smiled before moving on to the next student.

Derek looked at one final, then the other—95 and 97! He'd done even better than he'd hoped! "Hey, Parnell! Check these out!"

He showed Gary his marks, and Gary squinted through his glasses to get a better look. "Not too bad, Jeter. But not quite good enough." Gary's familiar, sneering smile emerged, and he held up his own test papers. "Ninety-six and ninety-eight. Read 'em and weep."

"Dang!" Derek said, smacking his hand down on his desk.

"Hey, listen. Don't get down on yourself. You did great," Gary said consolingly. "I'll bet you would have beaten me if you hadn't been going through some stuff."

Derek was surprised that Gary was aware of the situation with him and Dave.

"Thanks, Gar. You know, you surprise me sometimes."

"*You* surprised *me* last week," Gary said. "And I have to say, it made a big difference. So thanks right back at you."

"Hey, Gar, you want to come with us to the cages on Saturday? It's my birthday party, and we're going for pizza afterward." He hadn't planned on inviting Gary, but it just seemed like the right thing to do.

"I wish I could," Gary said. "But I've got karate that day."

"Oh. Too bad—I guess."

"Really. I still think it's dumb, even though I'm now a yellow belt. I could probably even flip you for real at this point. But you know what? I'm going to tell my mom I'd rather go to the cages instead. I'll bet she lets me come. All she cares about is that I get exercise."

"Cool! Let me know tomorrow?"

"Sure. And guess what else? I get two whole weeks off from karate, starting next week!"

"Math camp?"

Gary nodded. "The invitation's still open, you know."

Derek winced. "Maybe next year."

"Yeah, right. And maybe next year you'll actually beat me on a test or two."

Derek had to laugh. He should have known their little warm and fuzzy moment wouldn't last. Gary was who Gary was, and in the end that was who he would always be. Same kid next year as he was the year before.

He was a funny kind of friend to have, if you could call him a friend. But Derek was still glad he'd invited him. Gary was different for sure—but weren't he and Dave different too? And Vijay?

And everyone, if you really thought about it. *The differences between people are what make them interesting,* he thought. *Life wouldn't be much fun if everybody was exactly the same.*

They had their end-of-year party, the bell rang, and all the students of Saint Augustine's school walked out into the sunshine for the last time until September.

Derek felt deeply happy. There was one *huge* piece of unfinished business, and if it didn't go well, it would cast a huge shadow over everything else:

The team had to win the big game—they just *had* to!

The mighty Reds, champions of the East Side league, had compiled a regular-season record of 11–1, and they'd gone undefeated in their league's playoffs. And here, with the trophy game being held on the East Side, their fans were everywhere. The home bleachers were filled with people in red hats and T-shirts.

The Indians had some fans here too, mostly just the players' families, wearing their team's maroon and gray. Derek noticed that this time both of Dave's parents were here. That, more than anything else, told him things had definitely changed for the better.

"Everybody, remember to breathe," Coach Bradway told the team. "I know you're all excited, but you can't play your best unless you stay calm and don't let yourselves get rattled."

Derek's dad also had a few words for the Indians. "When we started this season, I knew we had our work cut out for us," he said. "But you boys have shown me something. You've worked hard, you've listened well, and you haven't let anything get you down. It's no accident that we're here today. And if we play our best game yet, it will be no accident when we hold up that big Kalamazoo Trophy!"

The Indians let out a yell. It made all the Reds turn and take notice. *Good,* thought Derek. *Let* them *be the ones who are nervous!*

Mason started the team off with a big base hit on the first pitch. But not content with a mere single, he was thrown out at second trying to stretch it into a double! It took a great throw from the center fielder to nail him, but the Reds hadn't gotten this far by being a bad team. Derek knew well enough to expect more of the same today.

Dean legged out a slow dribbler for a single, so Derek came up to bat with a man on base. After taking a strike, he let another pitch go by over his head—and just then Dean took off for second.

The catcher winged it straight to the base, and the second baseman tagged Dean on his arm. "Out!" called the umpire.

Derek winced, frustrated that his team had gotten two hits but now had no one on base. If he were going to drive in a run, he was going to have to hit the ball hard and far. He swung as hard as he could at the next pitch—but whiffed. The pitcher then finished him off with a curve-ball that froze Derek midswing. And that was that for the Indians in the first.

In the Reds' half of the inning, they made Dave work hard, fouling off pitch after pitch. He did finally get the first two outs, but the third hitter smashed one to right field for a double, and then the cleanup hitter singled him in, for a 1–0 lead.

Dave retired the side on a strikeout, and the score stayed the same until the top of the third inning, when, after two quick outs, Mason came up to bat.

Mason didn't look at all powerful, but he could hit a ball pretty far if he really got his body into it. Derek saw that the Reds were playing him too shallow in the outfield, not expecting him to hit it with any authority.

Mason must have seen it too, because he smacked the first pitch right over the left fielder's head. By the time the kid caught up to it, Mason was in at third with a triple!

It must have rattled the Reds' pitcher, because he then walked Dean, bringing Derek to the plate for the second time in the game.

Derek remembered how he'd struck out on that last curveball, a pitch that not many kids their age threw. He told himself to look for it again if the count got to two strikes.

Five pitches later the count was 3–2. Sure enough, here came the curveball—and Derek was ready for it. He held back, trying to time it just right, and laced a line drive to left center that split the outfielders. Mason and Dean were both able to score, and suddenly it was 2-1, Indians, with Derek standing on second base.

Dave then hit a long fly to center. Derek was sure it would drop in for a hit, but the Reds' outfielders were really good at their positions. The center fielder took a flying leap and caught the ball a few inches before it hit the ground to end the Indians' rally.

In their half of the third, the Reds took the lead right back, on a walk and a two-run homer. But their lead didn't last very long. In the top of the fourth, Tito homered to tie the game!

In the bottom of the fourth, the Reds finally started to wear Dave down. He hit the leadoff man, gave up two singles, and handed the lead back to the Reds. After a strikeout and a foul pop, he gave up a single, sending another runner home, for a 5–3 Reds lead—the largest lead of the game for either team!

Still, it was a real seesaw affair, and Derek was sure the Indians weren't through scoring. The problem was, the Reds were the home team here, which meant they got to hit last. In a game like this, that could make all the difference.

The next hitter cracked a wicked line drive, but Dean made a fantastic shoestring grab in center to end the inning. Now it was the Indians' turn to make some noise at the plate.

Miles came to bat first—subbing for Gary, who for once

seemed disappointed to be sent back to the bench. Miles was an even bigger kid than Gary and had a lot of power. But he also struck out a lot, as Derek well knew. And this Reds pitcher was tough.

Miles looked overmatched, swinging wildly at two pitches way out of the strike zone. But on the third pitch he managed to make contact. Not *much* contact but enough to send the ball rolling slowly down the third-base line.

The catcher leapt out to grab it, and the third baseman charged the ball too. With everyone yelling, they must not have been aware of each other—because they collided, and the ball stayed right where it was. Against all odds, Miles stood, smiling, on first base!

Mason came up again, and Derek could feel his and the rest of the Indians' hopes rising. Sure enough, seven pitches later, Mason walked for what seemed like the hundredth time this season, putting runners at first and second with nobody out!

Dean followed with a sharp grounder to third. The third baseman snagged it with a beautiful dive to his right. With one motion he stepped on the bag and then fired to first for a double play!

With two outs, and time running out for the Indians, Derek came up to the plate for what was surely the biggest at bat of the entire season. He knew that a single here would drive Mason in from second. Then it would be up to Dave to get a big hit to tie the game.

On the other hand, if Derek made an out here, the rally would be over. The Indians would still be two runs down, with only one more half inning to bat. But Derek refused to think about that. He wanted only positive thoughts running through his mind at this critical moment. He told himself to breathe, stay calm, and let the other team be the ones with the jumpy nerves.

Right. Easier said than done.

Derek looked out and saw how the fielders were playing him. The Reds, being from another league, didn't know much about the Indians, and vice versa. So they didn't know that Derek liked to hit the ball the other way—even on an inside pitch.

Derek let two balls go by, getting ahead in the count. He knew the pitcher would try to throw the next pitch right over the middle of the plate, and he was ready. He slapped the ball right over the second baseman's head for a single, and Mason ran all the way home for the Indians' fourth run!

Derek clapped his hands and got ready to try to steal second base. He knew he had to get into scoring position so that the Indians could tie the game back up with a single.

Standing in the coach's box at third base, Coach Bradway gave Dave the sign to take a pitch. Then he turned to Derek and gave him the steal sign.

Ready . . . set . . . *go!* As soon as the ball left the pitcher's hand, Derek was off and running. He didn't stop to look in at the catcher—he needed every split second he could get. The throw came in, and the tag came down. Derek's foot hit the fielder's glove and knocked the ball out of it before touching the bag!

"Safe!" the umpire called.

"What?" The shortstop, who'd put the tag on Derek, was enraged. "He was out! I got him right on the foot, and then he *kicked* the ball out of my mitt!"

The Reds' coach came out to argue with the umpire, pulling his player out of the way before the ump threw him out of the game. "Isn't that interference?" the coach asked the umpire.

"Clean play," the ump said, holding his ground. "His foot knocked the ball out of the mitt. What do you want me to say? That's baseball. It's a perfectly legal play."

"But that's so unfair!" the shortstop complained to his coach.

"Okay, Billy," said the coach. "Calm down. The umpires get to make the calls. There's nothing we can do about it. Now let's just buckle down and win this game!"

Derek felt glad that he hadn't been called out for interference. But it really *had* been a clean play. Runners had the right to slide into a base, and he hadn't been *trying* to knock the ball loose.

Dave was at the plate still, swinging his bat like he smelled blood in the water. The pitcher fired one in as hard as he could. It was low, at the knees—a hard pitch for most hitters, but not where you'd want to pitch Dave, with his golf-like swing.

But the Reds didn't know that, of course. They'd never seen Dave before this game. Dave walloped the pitch, sending it soaring high over the left fielder's head. Derek scored easily—and here came Dave, right behind him! The throw was late, and the Indians led again, 6–5!

The Indians and their fans erupted in cheers, while the big Reds crowd was silenced and stunned.

Tito popped out to second base to end the rally. But the Indians had the lead back now! The question was, in a game like this, with all its twists and turns, could they keep it?

It seemed that way to Derek after Dave mowed down the Reds in the bottom of the fifth. Three more Reds outs, and the Kalamazoo Trophy would be theirs!

The Indians went down quickly in their half of the sixth, with Paul, Jonathan, and Eddie making quick, easy outs. Derek took a deep breath. Finally, it had all come down to this last half inning.

For the bottom of the sixth, Coach Jeter sent Jonathan in to pitch, putting Dave at third in his place. Jonathan had a strong pitching arm, but he didn't have Dave's trick pitch—the changeup—to go with it.

The Reds hit him hard from the start. Their first batter hit a sharp grounder through the right side for a single. The next batter hit two screaming foul balls that just missed being doubles—then smacked a liner right at Derek!

Derek flinched, stuck out his glove—and grabbed it! Then, realizing that the runner had come too far off first base, he fired over to Tito to complete the double play.

Derek took off his glove and tried to shake the sting out of his palm. *Ouch! That one hurt!* Not that he cared. He'd gotten two outs, and saved at least one run—the run that would have tied the game back up.

Two outs now. Just one more to go. But in baseball no game is over till it's over. The next hitter clobbered one into center field for a double. Jonathan then walked the next two batters on just nine pitches, to load the bases!

Coach Jeter came jogging out to the mound. "Derek!" he called, signaling to the umpire that he was making a pitching change.

Last inning. Bases loaded. Two outs.

Derek realized that his dad was putting the entire game into Derek's hands. The fate of the entire team, the ending of their entire season, now rested on his shoulders.

Derek was determined not to let the team down. He was glad, in fact, to shoulder the burden. So what if he hadn't done much pitching? A ballplayer was a ballplayer. You did whatever your coaches called on you to do.

Everything he'd done, all that practice for all those years, had led him to this moment—and he was ready for it.

The Reds' cleanup hitter slowly waggled his bat, daring Derek to throw it over the plate. Derek took a deep breath and started off with a changeup. The hitter, cranked up to hit a fastball, swung early—and missed!

Strike one. Two more to go.

Derek got ready to throw a fastball now—but knowing how anxious the hitter was to swing, he threw it just outside. The batter made contact but fouled it off for strike two.

After throwing one into the dirt just to see if the hitter would bite, Derek wound up and fired another fastball—this one at eye level. It must have looked nice and fat, because the batter swung for all he was worth—and popped up to the infield!

Derek settled under it and made the catch that ended the game! They'd done it! They'd won it all! The Indians were the champions of all Kalamazoo!

All the Indians raced to join the pile and celebrate, while the devastated Reds slunk slowly off the field. Derek saw some of them slamming their mitts and caps onto the ground. He heard one kid say, "It's so *unfair*!"

Derek knew just how they felt. But he wasn't going to let that get in the way of his happiness. Not today. This had to be the greatest moment of his life so far!

At the ice cream celebration their coaches handed out trophies to every member of the team, saying something nice about how they'd improved during the season, and reliving all the great plays and key hits that had brought the team to ultimate victory.

Dave's parents were there too, sitting at a table with Derek's parents; Sharlee and her best friend, Ciara; and Chase. They all seemed to be getting along very well, which made Derek happy. The Hennums looked more relaxed than he'd ever seen them.

Dave came up to him as he was finishing his banana split, and made Derek's all-time happiest day even better. "Guess what?" Dave said. "My parents said I can come to New Jersey with you for a whole week this summer!"

"No way!" They slapped five every which way they could think of. "That is so awesome!"

Dave's announcement had come as a total surprise. Derek had planned on reminding him about the invitation. But obviously Dave hadn't forgotten about it after all. In fact, he'd just handed Derek the best birthday present ever!

Remember this moment, Derek told himself. He knew life wasn't always fair and that not every moment would be this happy. But for now he wanted to savor every second.

Here he was, a champion for the first time in his life! Even more important, he had not one but *two* best friends—and one of them was going to come with him for a whole week to his grandparents' house! Derek could picture them going to Yankees games together, playing ball with the local kids and his cousins in New Jersey. . . .

Then it occurred to Derek that there was one last thing—one more question that needed answering. One more thing to make this day absolutely, totally perfect.

He went over to his parents' table. "Hey, Dad?" he asked. "Do you think you could coach the team again next year?"

Mr. Jeter smiled, put a hand on Derek's shoulder, and gave it a squeeze. "I'll tell you what, Derek. I will if Coach Bradway will."

"Hey," said Chase, "I'd be up for that, Charles. We sure work well together as a team!"

Hmm, thought Derek, looking around at his Indians teammates, including his two best friends in the world. *I guess you could say that about* all *of us!*

INDIANS CHAMPIONSHIP GAME ROSTER

Mason Adams—2B

Dean O'Leary—CF

Derek Jeter—SS

Dave Hennum—P

Tito Ortega—1B

Paul Edwards—C

Jonathan Hogue—3B

Vijay Patel—RF

Gary Parnell—LF

Reserves: Miles Kaufman, Eddie Falk,
Jonah Winters
Coaches: Charles Jeter and Chase Bradway

JETER'S LEADERS

is a leadership development program created to empower, recognize, and enhance the skills of high school students who:

◎ **PROMOTE HEALTHY LIFESTYLES AND ARE FREE OF ALCOHOL AND SUBSTANCE ABUSE**

◎ **ACHIEVE ACADEMICALLY**

◎ **ARE COMMITTED TO IMPROVING THEIR COMMUNITY THROUGH SOCIAL CHANGE ACTIVITIES**

◎ **SERVE AS ROLE MODELS TO YOUNGER STUDENTS AND DELIVER POSITIVE MESSAGES TO THEIR PEERS**

Photo credit: Eileen Barroso/Turn 2 Foundation, Inc.

"Your role models should teach you, inspire you, criticize you, and give you structure. My parents did all of these things with their contracts. They tackled every subject. There was nothing we didn't discuss. I didn't love every aspect of it, but I was mature enough to understand that almost everything they talked about made sense." **—DEREK JETER**

DO YOU HAVE WHAT IT TAKES TO BECOME A
JETER'S LEADER?

- ◊ I am drug and alcohol free.
- ◊ I volunteer in my community.
- ◊ I am good to the environment.
- ◊ I am a role model for kids.
- ◊ I do not use the word "can't."
- ◊ I am a role model for my peers and younger kids.
- ◊ I stand up for what's right.

- ◊ I am respectful to others.
- ◊ I encourage others to participate.
- ◊ I am open-minded.
- ◊ I set my goals high.
- ◊ I do well in school.
- ◊ I like to exercise and eat well to keep my body strong.
- ◊ I am educated on current events.

CREATE A CONTRACT

What are your goals?

Sit down with your parents or an adult mentor to create your own contract to help you take the first step toward achieving your dreams.

For more information on JETER'S LEADERS, visit
TURN2FOUNDATION.ORG

BULLYING.
BE A LEADER
AND STOP IT.

Do your part to stop bullies in their tracks.

Protect yourself and your friends with STOPit. It's easy.
It's anonymous. It's the right thing to do.

"Never let a bully win." - Derek Jeter

Download the app today!

TURN THE PAGE FOR A SNEAK PEEK AT

CURVEBALL.

NEW YORK TIMES BESTSELLING AUTHOR

DEREK JETER

CURVEBALL

Crack!

As soon as the bat hit the ball, Derek knew it was coming his way. From his crouch he tracked the screaming liner with his eyes, timing his leap, upward and to his right. At the last instant he stretched his arm as far as he could.

It seemed to Derek in that nanosecond, as he flew through the air, that he really was flying! It also seemed to him that his arm extended farther than the possible limits of human arm-stretching. . . .

And the ball hit his mitt—right at the outer edge of the webbing! Derek squeezed the ball tightly as he fell back to earth, held it as he hit the dirt of the infield and kept skidding.

"Two! Two! Two!" someone was shouting at him. Derek knew what that meant. He had a chance to get the runner trying for second base, making two outs in one incredible play—if he could just get up and throw to second on time!

Somehow he got the throw off, and Willie Randolph grabbed it in his mitt. At that exact millisecond the runner slid into Willie's glove. "OUT!" the umpire yelled.

"Way to go, Derek!" shouted his best friend Dave from Kalamazoo, who was manning third base.

"Attaboy, Derek!" said Ron Guidry, the pitcher, congratulating him as they both stepped into the Yankees dugout. "Thanks for saving my bacon."

"Great play, kid!" Don Mattingly said, tipping his captain's cap.

Suddenly Derek found himself outside the stadium, in the parking lot. The game was over, but he was still in uniform. Next to him a car was gunning its engine—a sports car . . . and in the driver's seat, Dave Winfield. Derek's all-time favorite ballplayer!

"You played a great game today, kid," he told Derek as he gunned the engine. "Awesome job for an eleven-year-old."

HUH?

Eleven? What in the—

Derek sat up in bed with a start. *Wow,* he thought as he let his heart calm down in the darkness of the bedroom. *That was some dream.*

Across the room his sister, Sharlee, lay peacefully in

her bed, softly snoring. Derek looked over at the alarm clock. It was just after five in the morning.

Hearing the revving of a car motor, he realized that was what had woken him up. He went to the window. It was still dark outside, but at the far end of the yard, where the property met the road, his grandpa's old pickup truck was just pulling out of the long driveway.

Sharlee and Derek were spending the summer with their grandparents in Greenwood Lake, New Jersey, just as they did every year. And like on every other day while they were there, Grandpa was already on his way to work. Six days a week, and half days on Sundays too. That's what it was like to be the chief caretaker of a church, which was what Derek's grandpa had been for many, many years.

Grandpa always came home from work hungry and tired. Most evenings, all he could do was eat dinner, watch a little TV, and fall asleep—usually before Sharlee's bedtime, let alone Derek's. So it was mostly Grandma who was able to spend time with the kids.

She was the one in charge of the kids all day. She cooked for them, did the wash, cleaned the house, played with them, and tended to their cuts and bruises. The amazing part was, she almost always seemed to *enjoy* it. To Derek she had always been a kind of—well, not superhero, maybe, but superperson. She'd had thirteen kids of her own, including Derek's mom, and she'd raised them all into fine, upstanding grown-ups, and now she was helping watch all the grandkids, too. He hoped that when he was a grown-up, everyone would love and respect him the way everyone in the family did Grandma.

Derek looked out the open window. He could hear the crickets chirping. The sky was starting to get lighter.

He didn't feel the least bit tired. In fact, he felt restless. He couldn't wait for the morning to get going so that the usual fun could start!

He and Sharlee had already been here a few days, but it had rained a ton. They'd hung out a lot with their cousins, who all lived in the area, and some of whom always managed to end up sleeping over at Grandma and Grandpa's. They'd all gone bowling once, and to a movie another time.

But Derek hadn't been swimming in the lake much yet this summer—and that was where most of the fun happened around here.

Right now everyone was still asleep. Derek got dressed quietly, washed up, and went down to the kitchen to make a bowl of cereal, and wait for Grandma to come downstairs.

She was almost always the first awake, in order to make sure everyone's breakfast was ready before they even got downstairs, but she wasn't the first today. Grandpa's truck had seen to that by waking Derek up extra early. Still, Grandma was sure to be down in a few minutes, well before Sharlee, who usually slept till eight o'clock at least.

As he made "pre-breakfast" Derek thought back to the dream that had woken him up so early. What had been so great about it was that he and his friend Dave had been playing for the Yankees—the *real* Yankees, including Mattingly, Randolph, Guidry, and especially Dave Winfield.

Winfield had been a great player for years, and Derek idolized him. Derek knew everything there was to know about Winfield. Not just because he was a great ballplayer, but also because he was a great person. He'd even started his own charity!

Derek knew that, because he had done a report on Winfield last term at school, when they'd had to write about their role models—the people you look up to and listen to because you want to be like them in some way or other.

Derek had considered writing about his mom or dad, or grandma or grandpa. But his teacher had told them all to look for role models outside the immediate family. So Derek had chosen Winfield, naturally.

Derek hoped he could someday be like Winfield— except that he wanted to play shortstop for the Yankees, not right field. Derek felt deep inside that if he worked hard enough, and kept improving his game . . .

That was the thing that had been eating at him ever since he'd arrived for the summer. His game.

Sure, everything was great here in New Jersey, as usual. But Derek had just come off a great season of playing baseball, with his dad as his coach. They'd won the league championship—Derek's first title ever!

He'd been so psyched by the end of the season that he never wanted to stop playing ball. And as much fun as he always had with his grandma and grandpa, there was no summer Little League here that he could be a part of.

Derek feared he'd lose some of his new baseball skills over the summer. In fact, he wouldn't have another chance to get into a real game until Little League started up again next spring, almost a whole year from now.

Well, at least when Dave comes, Derek thought, *we'll be able to work on our game a little.* Dave was a good player, even though he'd been playing baseball for only a couple of years. Golf was Dave's real passion, and someday he hoped to go professional in that sport. For him baseball was just a way to have fun. But he had enough athletic talent that he could go far in baseball, too.

Derek knew why he'd seen Dave in the dream about the Yankees. Dave was going to be coming to visit him here in New Jersey in three weeks. Derek was psyched just thinking about it. He'd show Dave the lake, and the Castle, and introduce him to everybody, and get him involved in all the family fun.

The two of them would also find time, he hoped, to play some mini-golf, or pitch and putt—maybe even go to a driving range. Derek was sure he could persuade Grandma to take them.

Best of all, Derek was looking forward to taking Dave to his first major-league baseball game—at Yankee Stadium! Derek's grandmother always organized a family outing to a Yankees game every summer, always in early August, which was when Dave was due to be here.

The whole family came along, including Grandma, aunts, uncles, and cousins—even the little kids. It was always a blast. They practically took up a whole section in the upper deck in right field. Derek couldn't wait to share it all with his best friend in the world.

Or rather, with *one* of his *two* best friends. The other was Vijay Patel, but Vijay was in India for the whole summer with his family. They were there to attend a family wedding. Vijay hadn't been able to join Derek in New Jersey, but hey, there was always next year, right?

Grandma came into the kitchen just as Derek was finishing his cereal. "Well! Look who's the early bird!" she said with a chuckle. "Since when did you turn into an early riser?"

"I heard Grandpa's truck pulling out of the driveway."

Grandma frowned. "If I've told your grandpa once, I've told him a dozen times, to get that muffler fixed." She glanced at Derek's empty cereal bowl. "Aha! I see you've already made yourself breakfast. I guess you won't be wanting any of my homemade pancakes, then—"

"Yes! Yes, I want some!" Derek shouted, then put a hand

over his mouth. He hadn't meant to yell so loudly when everyone else was still asleep. Besides him and Sharlee, there were always other cousins staying at the house.

"Hmm," said Grandma. "I suppose I could let you have two breakfasts, just for today," she joked. "After all, you're a growing boy." She turned toward the pantry, going for the flour.

"Grandma, never mind. I can wait," Derek said suddenly, hopping out of his chair. "I want you to see how far I can hit the ball now! Come on out into the yard, and I'll show you!"

"It'll have to be a short session," she warned. "Aunt Dorien is coming at seven thirty to drop off Jessie and Alfie on her way to work, and I've got those pancakes to mix up for everyone."

Aunt Dorien worked in New York City, about an hour away by car. She was a manager at a hospital. Her kids, Jessica and little Alfie, were five and three years old. Grandma would be making pancakes for them, too, and then they'd all head over to the Castle for a day at the lake with the rest of the family.

Grandma Dorothy had lots of responsibilities, but her main one was watching all the family's kids all day while they played down at the lake, which was about a five-minute drive away.

The property belonging to Derek's extended family featured a huge old stone house, known as "the Castle" because it really did look like one. It had been built by some rich guy long ago but had since been made into several apartments, most of which were lived in by Derek's relatives.

There were other, smaller homes on the property too, as well as a large lawn leading down to the lake. Derek's cousins played all kinds of games on the lawn—volleyball, tag, touch football, soccer, and of course Wiffle ball, which always frustrated Derek.

He had cousins who were his age or older. But there were also lots of little kids running all over the place, so it wasn't safe to hit a baseball, or even a softball. And after years of playing hardball in Little League, Wiffle ball just didn't do it for Derek anymore.

There was a public beach in the town of Greenwood Lake, but the family members almost never went there. Why would they, when all they had to do was jump into the lake off the cement boat dock at the Castle? There was a wooden floating platform about a hundred feet out, where they could rest if they were tired, and pretend they were on a boat or a ship.

Yes, there was always someone to have fun with, just not this early in the morning.

"I should be making breakfast for the others," Grandma objected. "Sharlee and the rest will be up in a little while, if they aren't already."

"Don't worry. They'll yell when they want food. Here,

put this on," he said, giving her his mitt. "I'll hit 'em to you.

"I saw you hit some whoppers," said Grandma. "Down by the lake, when you were playing Wiffle ball the other day. You were really whacking that ball!"

"Wiffle ball?" Derek moaned. "Wiffle balls don't go far when you hit them. You've got to see me hit a real baseball!"

"And who's going to chase down all these home runs of yours?" she asked. But he was already jogging over to the far end of the yard, by the woods at the edge of the property. Grandma followed him. Raising his bat as she tossed the ball, he swung with all his might.

The ball dropped harmlessly to the ground behind him. He'd been in such a rush to show off for her that he hadn't remembered to keep his eye on the ball. "Wait, wait!" he said.

"I didn't see anything," she called. "Did you hit anything yet?"

He could see the grin on her face. Grandma loved to tease him. She loved all her grandkids and would have dropped everything to spend time with any of them. She'd been Derek's biggest fan ever since he could remember. Why, it was all because of her that he'd become a Yankees fan.

His second swing was right on the money. The bat hit the ball with a sharp *CRACK!* It sailed way past Grandma and right out onto the road. "Whoa!" she cried as she jogged carefully across to fetch it. "Who was that? Mickey Mantle? Joe DiMaggio?"

Derek laughed. On his next swing he hit one way over her head. It landed on the road and took a high bounce onto the neighbor's lawn across the street.

After she'd retrieved it, Grandma walked the ball back in. "Derek, we'd better have you hit it the other way, before you wind up denting somebody's car."

So they switched sides. That might have helped avoid an accident, but it didn't help Grandma any. Time after time she had to make her way into the woods to find the balls he'd hit past her.

"This yard isn't big enough for you anymore," she told him after six or seven swings, when she'd had enough of picking her way through fallen branches and underbrush. "We've got to find you another place to hit. Otherwise we're going to run out of baseballs mighty fast!"

"I told you I got better at hitting!" Derek said proudly. "I can field better too!"

"I'll bet you can." She put an arm around him. "But not before you have some pancakes in you." She kissed him on the forehead, and they went back into the house.

There was still no sign of Sharlee or the others, but once they smelled the pancakes, they'd be down in a hurry, Derek knew.

"You really have come a long way in one short year," Grandma told him as she mixed the batter. "I guess Wiffle ball doesn't quite do it for you anymore, like in the old days when you were little."

She poured the batter into the frying pan, and it sizzled, making a delicious smell. "Maybe when your friend Dave is here, you can get into a game or two over at the high school field. Logan and Andrew play softball over there sometimes."

Logan and Andrew were cousins of his who were in high school. Derek had already thought of asking them about it, but he wasn't really into softball either. For him it had always been hardball or nothing.

But her mention of Dave had reminded him of something else—he needed to ask her about Dave coming with them to Yankee Stadium on his visit. He was sure she'd say yes, but he'd already promised Dave, and he didn't want to leave it till the last minute to get permission from Grandma.

"Oh, by the way," she said, before he got a chance to open his mouth. "I forgot to tell you. I've made our reservations for the Yankees game, so keep your glove handy. We're going to see the Yankees play the Red Sox on Wednesday!"

"*Wednesday?* But that's only five days from now! And we always go in early August!"

"Well, that's usually true. But your uncle Louie and aunt Edna are going to Niagara Falls that week with their kids, and it wouldn't be the same without them. The more the merrier, right?" Louie and Edna had five kids, including Zach, their oldest, who was fourteen, and nine-year-old Oscar, the cousin who Derek always had the most fun with.

"But—but what about—" Derek blurted out before catching himself midsentence. He couldn't very well tell her, without checking with her first, that he'd *promised* Dave that he would get to see the Yankees.

Derek knew that his family went to only one Yankees game every summer. It was expensive, not to mention hard to arrange, what with so many cousins and aunts and uncles involved. But they had *always* gone in early August. He'd never even considered that Grandma might change the date.

Now Dave might not get to go to a Yankees game at all, and it would be all Derek's fault.

"Is there some problem, Derek?"

Derek didn't know what to say. He didn't want to seem ungrateful, and he knew it would be too much to ask Grandma to return all those tickets and start over again, making arrangements for twenty-five people to go to another Yankees game, and leaving out Zach and his whole branch of the family just so that Dave could come.

"Derek?"

He opened his mouth to speak, but he never got to say anything, because just at that moment Sharlee came bounding down the stairs, yelling, "Whoopee! Pancakes!"

And at the same moment he heard Aunt Dorien's car pulling into the driveway. Derek realized he'd have to wait till later to talk with Grandma about Dave and the Yankees game.

Which was just as well, because he had no idea what to say or do about it.